Maggie Sullivan was wearing an outfit worth waiting for.

But Luke was not the kind of guy who ~~could~~'d be trusted with a woman who ~~_____~~.
Let her go, his voice of re~~ason_____~~

"Hey, Maggie," ~~_____~~

She spun, start~~_____~~ ~~h~~adn't he just let her le~~ave_____~~

That's what I told y~~ou___~~ ~~th~~e voice of reason reminded him.

Maggie was trying very hard not to smile. But then it flickered across her lips, disappeared and then reappeared, like the sun peeping out of rain clouds.

The sun won and changed everything. Maggie's smile was wide and infectious. In the blink of an eye it transformed her from an old schoolmarm to a woman who looked young and carefree... and astoundingly beautiful.

How was it possible he'd been in such proximity to her earlier and hadn't noticed how kissable her mouth was?

Miss Maggie had lips that could be declared dangerous weapons. And he was determined to see them put to good use.

CARA COLTER

shares ten acres in the wild Kootenay region of British Columbia with the man of her dreams, a spirited teenage daughter, six spotted horses and a fiery orange tabby cat. Her perfect day includes writing, riding and reading. Cara has weaknesses for Tim Horton's iced cappuccino (a true Canadian pleasure), English toffee coffee, and high quality chocolate (the only known remedy for writer's block).

It is those weaknesses that have her waiting eagerly for NoWait, the weight-loss oil introduced in *The Greatest Risk*, to become a reality. "NoWait is every woman's dream. 'A little rub on the skin, and in no time you're thin!'"

Logan's Legacy

The Greatest Risk
Cara Colter

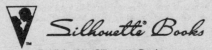

Published by Silhouette Books

America's Publisher of Contemporary Romance

Special thanks and acknowledgment are given
to Cara Colter for her contribution
to the LOGAN'S LEGACY series.

SILHOUETTE BOOKS

ISBN 0-373-61396-2

THE GREATEST RISK

Visit Silhouette Books at www.eHarlequin.com

Printed in U.S.A.

Be a part of

$\mathscr{L}$OGAN'S $\mathscr{L}$EGACY

*Because birthright has its privileges
and family ties run deep.*

**Two mismatched people meet and discover
an unquenchable passion. Can love be far
behind?**

Luke August: Whether it's scaling a tall building
or making daredevil jumps on his motorcycle, Luke
loved taking risks. But nothing prepared him for
Maggie Sullivan and the adventure she offered....

Maggie Sullivan: A dedicated social worker who
loved dealing with children and parents, Maggie
wanted a family of her own someday. She had no
intention of dating a thrill-seeker, but Luke was in
a league of his own when it came to excitement.

The Good Doctor? Dr. Richie had mysteriously
charmed the Portland community with his
weight-loss oil. Could this elixir be responsible
for the sudden surge of amorous behavior
among his followers?

THE SOLUTION YOU'VE BEEN WAITING FOR...

THE REMEDY YOU DESERVE...

NoWAIT

THE AMAZING NEW DIET OIL. USE IT AND WATCH THE POUNDS MELT AWAY!

NoWait: A little rub on the skin, and in no time you're thin!

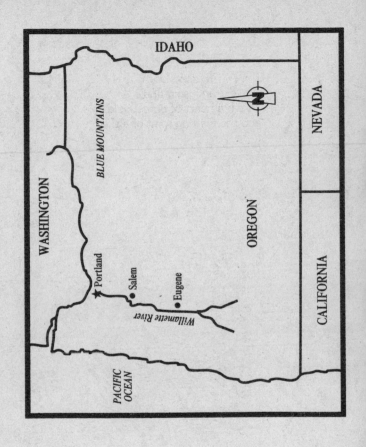

To Jane Leyh,
an inspiration,
with a heart of purest gold,
and the fighting spirit of a tiger

Prologue

They loved him.

Dr. Richard Strong stood on the front steps of *his* new clinic and looked out at the sea of upraised faces. All his life he had waited for this moment, and he stood in the glory of it, drank it in through his skin, felt as wholly and fully alive as he had ever felt.

Take that, Dr. Beachball, he silently addressed his TV nemesis, Dr. Terry Browell, a tubby psychologist with sparse red hair whose runaway success with the TV program "Live Airy with Dr. Terry" both baffled and frustrated Dr. Strong.

Richard knew he himself looked excellent for his forty-two years. He was trim and appealing. He ran a hand through his own thick silver-streaked dark hair. It was a gesture that he knew endeared him to audiences, making him look boyish and humble, as if he didn't quite know what to do next.

But of course he knew exactly what to do next.

"Under my leadership," he said, his voice strong and sure, "Portland General Hospital's new Healthy Living Clinic will be on the cutting edge of health and wellness. But we are not just about health." He paused dramatically. "We are about hope!"

The applause was thunderous, and he tilted his head and smiled, then turned slightly so that the TV news cameras caught his best profile. Maybe, one day soon, he would have his own television series! He was so much more suited for celebrity than dumpy Dr. Terry Eatwell.

The applause began to die, and Richard could feel it waning, as if it was stealing energy from him, so he stepped forward and cut the yellow ribbon. The renewed applause lifted him above his past mistakes, his self-doubts.

He studied some of the faces before him, and felt as though all that was less than perfect about him was being erased by the adoration he saw in these eyes.

He recognized Ella Crown, the aging florist from the hospital. Everyone secretly called her the dragon lady, but he had charmed her by buying her one of her own flowers, tucking it in the pure white of her hair. He doubted Dr. Terry would have been up to the task!

And there, standing close to Ella, was that plain social worker—Maggie, he thought her name was—from Children's Connection. The poor girl had never looked anything but tired and distracted to him, but now as she gazed up at him, he could see the hope he had just promised shining in her eyes.

Her beautiful redheaded friend stood beside her and she, too, was smiling approvingly. But instead of being taken by her beauty, Dr. Richard Strong remembered, a trifle uneasily, all the beautiful women who had been abandoned on his path to standing right here.

The applause was dying again. He could not allow the sudden intrusion of his past to steal this moment from him. Not when he had waited so long and worked so hard!

He looked behind him at the dignitaries and prominent hospital staff seated on the raised dais. How unfortunate that his eyes should meet those of Faye Lassen, possibly the only person he had not won over. She coveted the Chief of Staff position, he knew. *His* position. And she was eminently qualified, too, with a Ph.D. in nutrition and psychology.

But she had no presence. *Really, Faye,* he said to himself, *those glasses. Hideous.* Still, something in the deep, penetrating blue of those eyes was making his uneasiness grow.

He looked quickly away from Faye to public relations genius, Abby Edwards. Abby's lovely goldenbrown eyes held nothing but admiration for him.

It was quiet now as the audience waited. Dr. Strong wanted the love back. The silence was an empty void he was compelled to fill with his voice.

"I have a special surprise for all of you today," he announced. "To coincide with the opening of this leadingedge clinic, I am unveiling an amazing new product."

He liked the little murmur of anticipation. They thought he was just a motivational speaker, the latest health and fitness guru, but Richard's days of being underestimated were over. He was a scientist, an inventor, *a miracle worker.*

Really, he knew he should hold on a bit longer before releasing NoWait. The science on his new product was not quite as solid as it could have been. But he knew it worked! And he knew unveiling it would forever cement the admiration and adoration he felt from this crowd.

He'd already sent out several secret letters about the product to celebrities. Famous actress Cynthia Reynolds had answered him personally. Her interest promised him access to the world of fame and riches, promised him that finally he was going to matter.

He reached into his inside pocket, touched Cynthia's letter affectionately, and then pulled out the slim, gold box that had been nestled beside it. On it was a picture of him. The box was beautiful, a marketing marvel. But then he, Richard Strong, of all people, knew that packaging was everything. Packaging and the pitch.

"Ladies and gentlemen," he said, "I present to you NoWait, a pure homeopathic oil that guarantees weight loss." He paused and repeated, softly, "Guarantees."

He had their attention now. Dr. Richard Strong lowered his voice, felt the audience leaning toward him. "Unwanted pounds can vanish within hours."

He savored the gasp of the audience. "With the amazing NoWait oil, a woman can go from a size sixteen to a size six within one month."

The silence ended abruptly. Voices rose and fell in incredulous excitement. He held up his hand.

"NoWait," he repeated the name. "A little rub on the skin, and in no time you're thin." There was a ripple of appreciative laughter. He knew it was time to pull back.

"Please join me inside," Richard invited, "for a tour of the new facility."

The press was calling out questions. People were pushing forward. Flushed with the intoxicating power of success, Dr. Richard Strong passed out NoWait samples, accepted congratulations, gave thoughtful, intelligent answers to the press. Only he knew how often in his mind he had fielded those very questions.

They loved him. He could see it. He could feel it. He needed it.

Dr. Richard Strong would have been quite dismayed to learn there were two people in his audience not the least taken with him.

One, a curvy, attractive, middle-aged woman with shoulder-length blond hair had to hug herself against the chill she felt as she saw the crowds pushing toward the man she had once been married to, the father of her son.

"I know who you really are, Richard Strokudnowski," she whispered.

The other person who was not totally enamored with Dr. Richard Strong had happened by the ribbon-cutting ceremony by pure chance. He had been on his way to the main hospital building to see his ailing grandmother, and his way had been blocked by the crowd.

Resigning himself to the delay, he had listened with customary skepticism. But it was with growing alarm that he took in the looks on the faces in the crowd.

They were buying this nonsense. Well, why wouldn't they? The man was the new Chief of Staff of a branch of a medical institution with an impeccable reputation.

Narrowing his eyes on the man at the center of the

crush of attention, Detective Daniel O'Callahan folded his arms over the broadness of his chest.

"I know a snake-oil salesman when I see one," he muttered out loud.

The observation earned him dirty looks from several of the pudgy people around him. Still, Daniel made a quick mental note that the good doctor needed to be watched.

Which would take time, the commodity Daniel had the least of. He sighed and put Dr. Richard Strong on a back burner. But he knew he wasn't about to forget him.

One

"Excuse me," Maggie Sullivan said, trying to get by the couple who were blocking the main staircase into Portland General Hospital.

Sheesh, she thought to herself, *weren't they just a little old for that?* She glanced at them from behind a silky curtain of blond hair. She could feel herself blushing.

The woman was perhaps forty, coiffed, bejeweled and dignified in every way—except that she had her tongue tangled with that of a silver-haired man who was pressed so tightly against her that a piece of paper couldn't have been inserted between them.

To make matters worse, Maggie was sure she recognized the woman from the seminar that she and her best friend, Kristen, were taking at the recently opened

Healthy Living Clinic. The New You: Bold and Beautiful was being given by Dr. Richard Strong himself, which made it twice as appealing.

Maggie did not think the performance she was reluctantly witnessing was what Dr. Strong meant when he'd finished the seminar by giving them a homework assignment. He'd said, "Be bold. Do something totally out of character this week."

For Maggie that had meant eyeing up the bold and flirty red summer dress in the front window of Classy Lass, a haute couture shop way out of her price range.

"Excuse me," she said again, a trifle more forcefully.

The couple moved marginally, without unfastening their lips. Maggie slid by them, giving them a look of firm disapproval that she was pretty sure neither one of them saw.

Maggie, she told herself, don't be so judgmental. She did not know the story behind the obvious passion of that kiss. Maybe one of them was being admitted for a life-threatening illness or a complicated surgery. It would be okay to kiss like that if you thought you were saying goodbye forever. Wouldn't it?

At the top of the stairs, she paused and looked back on the situation, prepared to reevaluate it in this softer light.

The pins had fallen out of the woman's hair, and her silk jacket was halfway off her shoulder. She was running her knee up the man's thigh.

Maggie turned away from the scene so fast she bumped into the door. Dazed, she held her bruised nose, opened the door and hurried through it. Her face felt as if it was on fire. And, in truth, it wasn't just because she'd embarrassed herself by slamming full-force into a glass door. Nor was it entirely because of seeing the couple behaving so brazenly in public.

There was a tingle in the pit of her stomach that felt like hunger, only more intense. She felt as if she needed something, but with a type of need that was frightening, the kind of need she imagined a junkie must feel, or a gambling addict, or a person with the shakes reaching for a drink.

And she, Maggie Sullivan, was just not that kind of girl. In fact, she prided herself on the amount of control she had, on how responsible she was, how reliable.

But the truth was, this feeling had been enveloping her at odd moments for days. It had nearly overwhelmed her when she saw a young couple holding hands, when she overheard a whispered "I love you" in the hospital cafeteria, when she saw a man and a woman pushing a stroller. On those occasions, Maggie would feel an emptiness so vast, a yearning so strong, she felt as though the emotions could overtake her entire well-ordered life.

"I'm twenty-seven," she murmured. "Biological clock."

Unfortunately not a single soul had warned her that the ticking of a biological clock could seem much more like the ticking of a time bomb—as if it could explode without warning, leaving nothing but wreckage where a neat and tidy little life had once been.

Maybe biological clocks were something she needed to talk to Dr. Strong about at the next meeting of the B&B Club, as she and Kristen had dubbed the Bold and Beautiful series. B&B was the first in a full schedule of wellness seminars that Dr. Strong would be personally hosting.

Since she was still rubbing her nose from her last moment of inattention, Maggie really should have known better than to crane her neck for just one little last glance back. The couple was still on the steps. The man was gnawing on the woman's neck, and she was bent backward over his arm as if they were executing a very complicated dance maneuver. Maggie's head spun, as if she would die to feel that way, so enamored with another person that she could forget all the rules, enter a world of just two and never mind who was watching.

"Look out!"

Maggie whirled. Her mouth opened in shocked surprise, but no sound came out. A wheelchair was careening toward her at full tilt. A man was in it, his powerful shoulders drawn forward, his arm muscles gloriously knotted from the effort of propelling himself forward at such an atrocious speed.

She was aware of images—astonishing green eyes narrowed in ferocious concentration, thick dark-brown hair flying back, coppery unblemished skin beaded with sweat—and then Maggie awakened to the reality that she was about to be run down. She threw herself to one side to avoid being flattened.

Unfortunately the wheelchair veered crazily at exactly the same moment and in exactly the same direction. Maggie was lifted off her feet, the blow cushioned somewhat by bands of steel wrapping around her and pulling her hard into the wall of an extraordinary chest.

For a suspended moment it seemed as if a fall might be averted, but the wheelchair tilted, lolled, tried to right itself, listed crazily again and then capsized, dumping

Maggie on the floor and the wheelchair's inhabitant right on top of her.

The bands of steel—which she recognized were a deliciously masculine set of arms—remained wrapped protectively around her. She was remarkably unhurt, pinned below a strange man.

He was big and he was gorgeous. From her position, sprawled below the muscle-hardened length of his body, Maggie stared up at him, amazed. She ordered herself to sputter indignantly, but no sound came from her mouth.

Instead, she studied his eyes and decided she had never seen eyes that shade before, the exact color of those mysterious Mount Hood National Forest lakes that gleamed in smoky jade. The man's eyes were lit with equal parts of mischief and pure seduction, and fringed with a sinful and sooty abundance of black lashes.

Maggie used being stunned as a result of the collision to continue to stare at him. Her gaze drifted hazily down his features, ticking them off—thick, dark hair, arched eyebrows, beautiful nose except for a savage scar across the bridge, high cheekbones, strong chin. The cheeks and chin were darkly whisker-roughened. It was the face of a man who would have been far better suited to guide a pirate ship than a wheelchair.

But pity never entered her mind because his lips, full and firm, suddenly formed themselves into a sardonic grin that revealed teeth so brilliant and white and sexy that she felt the breath was being drawn from her body. This close she could even see the smile was not perfect—a chip was missing from the right front tooth—but it did not detract from the powerful male potency of that smile even one little bit.

Slowly, her awareness of the pure and roguish appeal of his face was diluted by another awareness. Their bodies were pressed as closely together as were those of that couple she had just judged on the front steps. And she was just as reluctant to pull away.

He was all hard edges and formidable masculinity, and Maggie could feel herself melting into him. She could feel the steel-band strength of the muscled arms that had tightened around her, protecting her from the worst of the fall. To her dazed mind, he felt good, heated and strong, the exact drug that unnamed yearning in her had craved. His scent enveloped her, tangy and tantalizing, the scent of wild, high places, forests and mountains, and all things untamed.

"Sorry," he said, but the lazy grin said he wasn't the least bit sorry, that he was quite content to be lying on the shiny tile floor of the main foyer of Portland General Hospital pressed intimately into the curves of a complete stranger.

"Oh!" Maggie said, coming to her senses abruptly. She could feel her skirt—marginally too tight, despite her faithful use of Dr. Strong's miracle NoWait ointment—binding the top of her thighs. She tugged frantically at it, not unaware that the lazy amusement burning in his eyes deepened as she wriggled beneath him.

She was, however unintentionally, putting on a better show than the couple outside. At least that couple probably knew each other.

"Anything I can help you with, ma'am?" he drawled.

"Oh!" Maggie said. "How impertinent!"

She rolled out from under him and onto her knees. The skirt was indeed stuck. She should have never taken Dr. Strong's advice to use only half doses of NoWait oil.

"You are already nearly the perfect size, my dear," he had explained to her, his sincere brown eyes making her feel as if she was the most beautiful woman in the world. "Apply a half dose of the oil behind your ears for its nutritional value."

If she'd taken the full dose, her skirt wouldn't be bunched up around her hips and refusing to move.

Her attacker's grin had evolved into a deep chuckle. If he wasn't wheelchair-bound, she would probably hit him for that chuckle, and for the frank and insolent way he was evaluating parts of her legs that, to date, had only been shown at the beach.

"Impertinent," he repeated slowly, as if he was trying on a new label to see if he liked it. She suspected he did.

She frowned disapprovingly at him.

"Are you okay?" he asked, propping himself up on one elbow. His eyebrows arched wickedly as if he had taken a front-row seat at the peep show.

"No, I am not okay," she said through clenched teeth. "I am exposing myself to half the hospital!"

He suddenly seemed to get it that she was not finding this situation nearly as amusing as he was. He shoved himself upward and then leaped lightly to his feet. He held an arm down to her.

She stared at him, astonished, as if he was a biblical character who had folded up his cot and walked.

"You aren't handicapped!" She ignored his arm and rocked back from her kneeling position to sitting, hoping that changing position would help her untangle the skirt where it bound her legs. The skirt, however, was determined to thwart her. When she got home tonight, she was rubbing a whole bottle of NoWait behind her ears!

He folded arms over a chest she now saw was massive. He had on a blue hospital gown that bound the muscles of his arms as surely as her skirt was binding her thighs, his result being far more attractive than hers. Underneath the gown, thank God, he had on a faded pair of blue jeans. He watched her undignified struggles with infuriating male interest.

"It's against the law to pretend to be handicapped," she told him, though she had no idea if it was or not.

"Handicapped?" He followed her glance to the overturned wheelchair. "Oh, that."

He watched her for a moment longer, then, apparently unable to stand it, moved quickly behind her and without her permission put his hands under her armpits and set her on her feet.

For some ridiculous reason an underarm deodorant jingle went through her head. She hoped, furiously, ridiculously, she wasn't damp under her arms.

"You were driving like a maniac," she said, yanking herself away from him to hide her discomfort at how it had felt to be lifted by him, so easily, as if she were a feather, as if the NoWait could gather dust in her bathroom cabinet forever.

"And you weren't watching where you were going," he said, coming back around to face her, looking down at her, smiling with an easy confidence and charm that might have made her swoon if he wasn't so damned aggravating.

She glared at him. She bet that smile had been opening doors—and other things—for him his entire life.

How dare he be so incredibly sexy, and so darned sure of it?

"Are you saying this was my fault?" she demanded.

"Fifty-fifty?" he suggested with aggravating calm.

"Oh!"

"Mr. August!"

He turned toward the voice. Maggie turned, too. Hillary Wagner, a nurse Maggie knew slightly from her own work as a social worker at Children's Connection, an adoption agency and fertility clinic that was affiliated with this hospital, was coming toward them, looking very much like a battleship under full steam.

Apparently here was a woman who was immune to the considerable charm radiating off Mr. August. "What on earth have you been up to now?"

"Remember the nurse from *One Flew Over the Cuckoo's Nest?*" he asked Maggie in an undertone.

Maggie sent him a look. Was he an escapee from the psych ward, then?

Hillary took in the upturned wheelchair, and her tiny gray eyes swept Maggie's disheveled appearance.

"Mr. August, you've been racing the wheelchairs again!" she deduced, her tone ripe with righteous anger. "And this time you've managed to cause an accident, haven't you?"

"Yes, ma'am," he said, and hung his head boyishly, but not before giving Maggie a sideways wink.

"Mr. August, really! You cannot be racing wheelchairs down the hallways. Who were you racing with? Don't tell me it was Billy Harmon."

"Okay. You won't hear it from me."

"Don't be flip, Mr. August. He's a very ill boy. Which way did he go?"

"I think I caught a glimpse of him wheeling off that way in a big hurry when I had my, er, collision. Frankly, he looked better than I've ever seen him look, not the least ill."

"You are not a doctor, despite that horrible prank you pulled, visiting all the poor ladies in maternity."

"Isn't impersonating a doctor illegal?" Maggie asked.

"It certainly is!" Hillary concurred.

But he ignored Hillary and turned to Maggie, not the least chastened. "What are you—a lawyer? I wasn't impersonating a doctor. I found a discarded lab jacket and a clipboard. People jumped to their own conclusions."

"You are a hazard," Hillary bit out.

"Why, thank you."

"It wasn't a compliment! Billy is sick, Mr. August, and even if he wasn't, wheelchair racing is not allowed. Do you understand?"

"Aye, aye, mon capatain, strictly forboden." He managed to murder both the French and German languages.

Maggie wanted to be appalled by him. She wanted to look at him with the very same ferocious and completely uncharmed stare that Hillary was leveling at him.

Unfortunately, he made her want to laugh. But it felt to Maggie as if her very life—or at least her professional one—depended on hiding that fact.

Hillary drew herself to her full height. "I could have you discharged," she said shrilly.

"Make my day," he said, unperturbed by her anger. "I've been trying to get out of this place for a week."

"Oh!" she said. She turned to Maggie. "Are you all right? Maggie, isn't it? From Children's Connection? Oh dear, your skirt is—"

"Very attractive," Mr. August said.

The skirt continued to be bound up in some horrible way that was defying Maggie's every attempt to get it back where it belonged.

Strong hands suddenly settled around her hips, and Maggie let out a startled little shriek.

The hands twisted, and the skirt rustled and then fell into place.

Maggie glared at the man, agreed inwardly he was a hazard, and then patted her now perfectly respectable skirt. "I don't know whether to thank you or smack you," she admitted tersely.

"Smack him!" Hillary crowed, like a wrestling fan at a match, without a modicum of her normal dignity.

"There's Billy," the hazard said.

Maggie turned to see a young man, perhaps fifteen or sixteen, his head covered in a baseball cap, doing wheelchair wheelies past the nurses' station. Giving Mr. August one more killing look, Hillary turned and dashed after Billy.

"Maggie, I'm Luke August."

Maggie found her hand enveloped in one that was large and strong and warm. She looked up into eyes that were glinting with the devil.

She snatched her hand away from his, recognizing the clear and present danger of his touch.

"You were racing wheelchairs?" she asked, brushing at an imaginary speck on her hopelessly creased skirt. "With a sick child?"

"He's not really a child. Seventeen, I think."

"And the sick part?"

"Careful, when you purse your lips like that you look just like Nurse Nightmare over there."

"I happen to be an advocate for children," she said primly.

"You would have approved, then. The kid's sick. He's not dead. He needs people to quit acting like he is. Besides, I was bored."

She stared at him and knew that he would be one of those men who was easily bored, full of restless energy, always looking for the adrenaline rush. He was the type of man who jumped out of airplanes and rode pitching bulls, in short, the kind of man who would worry his woman to death.

"What brings you to Portland General, Mr. August?" she asked, seeking confirmation of what she already knew.

"Luke. Motorcycle incident. Broke my back. Not as serious as it sounds. Lower vertebrae."

"Not the first time you've been a guest here?" she guessed.

He smiled. "Nope. They have my own personal box of plaster of paris put away for me in the E.R. I've broken my right leg twice, and my wrist. Of course, then there are the injuries they don't cast—a concussion, a separation and a dislocation. And the cuts that required stitches. That's what happened to my nose."

She suspected he knew exactly how darn sexy that ragged scar across his nose was, so she tried not to look. And failed.

He smiled at her failure, and that smile was devastating, warm and sexy. Of course, he was exactly the kind of man who knew it, and whom a woman with an ounce of sense walked away from. No, ran away from. He had mentioned seven injuries in the span of seven seconds!

Besides, he was exactly the kind of man who could have you breaking all the rules—kissing on the front steps of a public place and loving it—before you even knew what had hit you.

"Look, Maggie, it was nice running into you."

A different person might have known how to play with that, but she just looked at him with consternation.

"I'm trying to say I'm sorry I ran you down. Let me know if there's anything I can do to make it up to you," he said. He was dismissing her.

It was a carelessly tossed-out offer. He didn't mean it, and of course there wasn't anything he could do to erase the fact that she had been wagging her upper thighs at everyone who had come in the main entrance in the last few minutes.

But for some reason, looking into the jewel-like sparkle of those green eyes, feeling the wattage of that devilish grin, Dr. Strong's homework assignment came to mind.

Be bold. Do something totally out of character.

It would be absolute insanity for Maggie to actually say the words that formed in her brain. She thought of that couple kissing on the steps and was filled with a sudden, heady warmth.

"You could go out with me," she said, and then at the look of stunned surprise on his face, she stammered, "You know, to make it up to me."

His eyes widened, and then narrowed. He was looking at her in a brand-new way, and she suddenly had the awful feeling she was coming up short.

She was not the kind of woman a man like this dated. He dated women who had waterfalls of wild hair, who wore skimpy clothing molded proudly to voluptuous curves. He dated women who wore bright-red lipstick and had a matching color for their fingernails.

Fingernails that would be long and tapered, not short and neatly filed. Maggie hid her fingers behind her back, but it didn't help.

Maggie Sullivan was not Luke August's kind of woman and they both knew it. Still, why did her heart feel as if it was going to fly right out of her chest while she waited for his answer?

You could go out with me.

Luke eyed the woman in front of him with surprise. She did not look like the type of woman who surprised a man.

She was presentable enough, in that kind of understated way that he associated with schoolteachers, librarians and dental hygienists, though her eyes prevented her from being ordinary. They were a shade of hazel that danced between blue and green. She had beautiful blond hair, untainted by the color streaks that were so fashionable. Her features, her nose and cheekbones and chin were passably cute, but not spectacularly attractive.

And she had a nice body under that prim gray straight-line suit with the uncooperative skirt, and he knew quite a bit more about her body than he should, since it had been flattened under him for fifteen or twenty most delectable seconds.

But Luke had already guessed quite a lot about her from their short acquaintance. She would be the predictable sort. If she said she'd meet you at two, she was the type who would be there five minutes before. The problem with the predictable sort was they always had an expectation that you were going to share their predictability.

He also guessed she would prefer reading a novel to experiencing real adventure. Her idea of a perfect Friday night was probably to be curled up on her couch with a book, a cup of tea and a cat. The problem with that type was that they generally held old-fashioned values of home and family in high esteem, a view that, given his own childhood home life, he was not inclined to share.

He was willing to bet she was the type who could be counted on to bake cookies and bring them into the office, and even though Luke liked homemade cookies as much as the next man, he was wary of what they represented—a longing for domesticity.

If the woman in front of him was all that she appeared, she was sweet, wholesome and predictable.

In fact, not his type at all. Least likely ever to wreck a wheelchair while racing down a hospital corridor.

Also least likely to ask a strange man out. Were there more surprises lurking behind that mask of respectability? Damn. He did like the unexpected.

Still, when he'd asked if there was anything he could do for her, what he'd meant was that he'd pick up her dry-cleaning bill. He should have been more clear about that.

He was going home to his ideal woman in a few more days. Her name was Amber. She had long, wild, red-tinted hair, red lips and eyes that were so black they smoked. A lacy white bra, filled to overflowing, peeped out from under her black leather jacket.

Amber had appeared in his life—unexpectedly—in

April of 2002. In fact, she had appeared at the flick of his wrist. He'd been changing the calendar from March, and there she was, April 2002 on his Motorcycle Maidens calendar.

At least he was faithful to her. He had never turned the page to May. New calendars were a dime a dozen, after all, but a woman like Amber? He'd been searching for her since then. When he found her, then and only then, would he consider giving up the bachelor lifestyle. Meanwhile, he could tell his mother who, after seeking counseling several years back, had started showing unexpected and not entirely welcome interest in him, that he was "seeing" someone.

Amber was not the type who baked cookies, or was content with a cup of tea on a Friday night. She probably didn't like cats or small children. But the way she unbuttoned her jacket and leaned over the handlebars of that Harley—the exact same make, year and model that he himself rode—who cared?

Meanwhile, it was true, he'd gone through a number of Amber look-alikes. Big-busted redheads, with steamy smiles and promising eyes, some of whom even shared his addiction to all things fast and furious. But somehow it always dead-ended, always disappointed, never even got close to filling *that place*.

Luke did not like thinking about *that place*. The restless place. The empty space. He was thirty-four years old and facing up to the fact that the older he got, the harder it was to fill. Speed didn't do it anymore, not the way it used to. And the broken bones took longer to mend than they used to.

"What do you mean, go out?" he asked, leaning toward

her, playing the game he knew how to play. Even though she was not his type, the man-woman thing was an effective form of outrunning *that place*, at least temporarily.

She actually was blushing a charming shade of crimson, something Amber did not do, and would not do when he finally found her.

"Never mind," she said, and tossed her hair. "That was a silly thing to say. I don't know what got into me."

It was the wrong kind of hair for him. Since Amber, he liked redheads, and not necessarily real redheads, either. But that self-conscious toss had drawn his eye. Miss Priss's hair was an intriguing shade somewhere between corn silk and ripening wheat.

Considering it wasn't the type of hair he went for, at all, he found it odd that he suddenly wanted to touch it. "We could," he said, "go out."

Her green-blue eyes got very big. Amber would have licked her lips and let her eyes travel suggestively down his hospital gown, but hers didn't.

"Maggie, wasn't it? Isn't that what Nurse Nightmare called you?" He was helping her along, giving her an opportunity to flirt, but she was obviously terrible at this. She was looking everywhere but at him.

"Maggie Sullivan," she confirmed reluctantly. "But really, never mind."

"Go out?" he prodded her. "Like for a drink or something?"

"Oh. No. I mean I don't drink."

Hell's bells, this was getting worse by the moment. Amber would drink. Get on the tables and sway her hips and lick her lips when she'd had a few too many.

And he'd be the one who got to bring her home.

"So, what did you mean, then, go out?"

"I thought maybe a movie…or something," she said lamely.

Worse than he thought. A movie, which meant the big debate. Do you hold her hand? Put your arm over her shoulder? When was the last time going out had meant that to him?

He thought he'd been twelve.

"Did you have a particular movie in mind?" Mind. Had he lost his? Maggie Sullivan was not his kind.

On the other hand, his search for Amber was proving futile. Why not entertain himself until she came along? Maggie was the kind of girl who had always snubbed him in high school, the kind of girl lost behind too many books in her arms, not amused by being tripped by his big foot sticking out in the hall.

Miss Goody Two Shoes and the Wild Boy.

Life had been getting a little dull. Why not play a bit? She'd asked, not him. She'd started it. If she wanted to play with fire, why not accommodate her?

"I had heard *Lilacs in Spring* was good, but—"

Lilacs in Spring. He was willing to bet it was all about sappy stuff, no motorcycles or pool tables in the script. Kissing. Romance. Eye-gazing. Hand-holding. Fields full of flowers. Mushy music. In other words, the big yuck.

The type of movie he and Amber would not go to, ever.

"Meet me right here, at say, eight?" he said. "We could catch the late show."

"Aren't you in the hospital?"

"Did you ever see the movie *Escape from Alcatraz?*"

"No."

That figures. "Everything's way more fun when you're not supposed to do it," he explained, attempting to be patient with her. "I loved playing hooky as a kid. There are things a man misses about being a kid."

He could tell she just wanted to turn and run. She had never gone out with the kind of guy who liked playing hooky, not in her entire life. Instead she yanked her skirt down one more time, lifted her chin and said, "Eight o'clock it is."

She scurried away and he watched her, amused. "I bet I'll never see her again," he said out loud. Just the same, he knew he would be waiting here at eight o'clock just in case Miss Maggie Sullivan decided to surprise him one more time.

Something hit him hard in the knees and he turned around. Billy Harmon grinned at him from his wheel-chair. His bald head was covered with the baseball cap Luke had given him yesterday.

The kid just tugged at his heartstrings, a surprise to Luke, since he liked to deny the existence of a heart.

"Hey, Billy, you escaped Nurse Nightmare. Good man!"

"Luke, I got two rolls of toilet paper. You want to do something with me?" Billy leaned forward, his eyes alight with glee as he laid out his plan for laying a toilet-paper trail all the way from Nurse Nightmare's private bathroom facilities to the men's locked ward.

Luke scanned the boy's face, looking for signs of weariness, but there were none. That nurse had been right, he wasn't a doctor. But he knew mischief could be a tonic, especially for a kid who knew way too much about the hard side of life. In Luke's evaluation, Billy needed his mind taken off the bleak realities he faced everyday, and that wasn't going to happen if he was lying in bed staring at the ceiling.

"I'm in," Luke said, picking his wheelchair up off the floor. He inspected it for damage, found none and settled himself in the seat. He followed Billy's example and hooked the toilet paper roll on the back push grip where it began to unroll merrily behind him.

But the whole time he laid his toilet paper trail down the hall, Luke August was uneasily aware that he was thinking of eyes that were an astonishing shade of blue and green, not the least little bit like Amber's.

He tried to imagine if those eyes would be laughing or disapproving if she was watching him right now.

Who cares? he asked himself roughly.

He realized he did. And that maybe he was the one who needed to be thinking long and hard before he showed up in that hospital foyer at eight tonight.

Two

Luke caught a glimpse of his reflection in the glass of the hospital front doors, and felt satisfied with what he had accomplished. He was wearing the green overalls and the white-bill cap of a hospital custodian.

"Evenin', Doc," he greeted his own doctor as she hurried by him out of the building. She was an Amazon of a woman, in her mid-fifties, but they were on a first-name basis, and she had *that* gleam in her eye whenever she saw him. What could he say? It was a gift.

But tonight she barely glanced his way. "Good night," she said politely.

It wasn't just that she hadn't recognized him. It was as if he was invisible. People leaving the hospital as the end of visiting hours approached bustled by him in the main foyer with nary a glance, returning his casual greetings without really seeing him.

Invisible. Exactly the effect he had been attempting when he had raided the maintenance closet on his floor. Luke swabbed the floor with his mop and congratulated himself on his ease with the art of disguise. He liked trying on other personas and slipped into them easily.

He would have made an excellent spy or undercover cop, he thought. He realized he probably would have excelled in a career in acting. In fact, he had entertained the idea of becoming an actor after one successful role in a high school production. A girlfriend had talked him into playing Hook in *Peter Pan* and he had gotten a great deal of mileage out of telling his upscale and very conservative parents he planned to hit Hollywood upon graduation. He could not find a single other career choice that his parents disapproved of as heartily as that one, which was guaranteed to get a rise out of them both.

His eventual choice, a career in construction, had certainly proven to be a close enough second in the disapproval rating. Nevertheless, he hadn't looked back.

"Manly, too," he muttered to himself of his career choice. Now, though, he enjoyed being in character, an eccentric floor cleaner who muttered and swabbed. No one watching would be even remotely aware that Luke kept a surreptitious eye on the front door.

"Visiting hours are now over," the tinny voice over the public address system announced officiously.

Luke glanced at the clock, confirming what he had just heard. Eight o'clock, on the dot.

"Big surprise," Luke said to his washtub, giving the mop a vigorous wring. "Miss Maggie Sullivan, an on-the-dot kind of gal if there ever was one, is not coming."

After his weak moment this afternoon, when he had

caught himself actually *caring* what Miss Maggie would think of a grown man unraveling toilet paper down a hospital corridor, Luke had arrived at the conclusion that he was not going out with her. There was something dangerous brewing under the surface of that pristine exterior.

Still, as the hands of the clock had ticked closer and closer to eight, curiosity, that worst of male vices, had gotten the better of him.

He'd found everything he needed in the maintenance closet on his floor, including a name tag that said Fred. It was really the best of both worlds—he got to see if she showed up without being the least bit vulnerable himself.

Really, Luke told himself, it was as if he was studying human nature, nothing more. He wanted to see how accurately he had judged her character, and now he congratulated himself on his astuteness.

He'd surmised Miss Maggie had never asked a man out before in her life. He had predicted she would get cold feet.

Okay, he might have also been just a tiny bit curious what she would have worn had he happened to be wrong.

But he wasn't. He looked at the clock again. Three minutes after eight. If she was coming, he would have bet his last fifty cents she would have been here at precisely five minutes to eight. She was not the kind of woman who would be late. He knew these things. He should have let Billy in on it. They could have bet five bucks, though it would have been a shame to take Billy's money.

Just underneath the hearty round of congratulations

he was giving himself as he wrung out the mop one final time and prepared to go back to his room, Luke became aware of something besides self-congratulation stirring in his breast.

He realized he was wringing the mop just a little too vigorously, the handle bending dangerously under the pressure he was applying. He paused and analyzed the unwanted feeling that hovered at the edges of his consciousness. Could it be?

Disappointment?

No! He would never be disappointed because a little mouse like that had stood him up! Or if he was, it was only because he had gone to a great deal of trouble to be able to have a front-row seat to her reaction to being stood up by him.

He felt the cool draft of the front door opening, and out of the corner of his eye caught a flutter of movement. He turned his head marginally, froze, then ducked his head and began mopping again. He slid another glance out of the corner of his eye.

Her.

He waltzed the bucket around so he was facing her, but kept the bill of his cap down. He peered at her from under it and digested the fact the little mouse, Miss Maggie, had managed to surprise him again.

She had not been five minutes early. And she was not a no-show, either.

Maggie Sullivan stood, a trifle uncertainly, scanning the foyer. The outfit was worth waiting for. It was evident she had worked very hard at choosing it, and had arrived at a look that was not in the least overstated, and that was certainly not designed to impress anyone. Still, there was no denying the way those plain black trousers, flared faintly from knee to ankle, hugged the lovely feminine swell of hip that had caused her so much trouble earlier in the day. She had on a light-brown suede jacket over a black T-shirt that promised to be formfitting if he ever had an opportunity to get a better look at it.

He remembered the soft press of that form just a little too well.

"Brilliant," he muttered at the murky water in his bucket. The girl was obviously brilliant. She had chosen an outfit designed to make it look as though she was not trying to impress anyone, least of all not him, and that had succeeded in intriguing, nonetheless.

It was not an Amber-approved outfit. No cleavage or glimpses of underwear were to be seen, but it was a long way from the Miss Priss he had knocked right off her feet this afternoon. Her blond hair was free and cascaded down over her shoulders in a shiny wave. He felt that same rebel need to touch it that he had felt this afternoon.

He tried to read her features, but the little tilt of her delicate nose, the furrow at her brow and the quick glance at her watch were not all that readable.

Was she disappointed that he hadn't showed? He was amazed that he couldn't tell. She glanced at her watch, took another look around, then spun on her heel. He thought maybe he had caught a quick glimpse of something on her face before she had turned away. Relief?

That Luke appeared not to have shown up? That seemed unlikely, especially since she herself had gone to the trouble of getting here.

Still, she was leaving. Would she give up that

quickly? He had been at his station, a patient patient, for a full half hour.

Wait. Her shoulders slumped marginally as she pushed at the door. In that one small gesture he read a heartrending weariness at the ways of the world, and at the callousness of his sex.

He was not the kind of guy who could be trusted with a girl who got hurt easily, and he was the least likely guy to save his sex from a reputation of being callous. In fact, he had probably personally helped his gender gain that reputation!

Nope, Luke August knew himself inside out. He was superficial and insensitive, and for the most part, damned proud of it.

Let her go, his voice of reason cautioned him.

"Hey, Maggie." It was his other voice.

She spun, startled, and scanned the room again. Her eyes rested on him briefly, studied the empty foyer, and then returned to him, understanding dawning in them.

He rested his hands on the top of the mop, pushed the bill of his cap up with the handle and grinned.

She stared at him, her hand still on the door. It occurred to him that she was considering bolting, and that he would be sorry if she did. But then she let go of her grip on the door, turned, folded her arms over her chest and tapped her foot.

In that pose, she reminded him of a teacher he'd had in the sixth grade. A formidable woman whom he had not liked one little bit. Why hadn't he just let her leave?

That's what I told you to do, the voice of reason reminded him churlishly.

It occurred to him that underneath that stern expression, Maggie was trying not to smile. But the smile flickered across her lips, disappeared and then reappeared again, the sun peeping in and out of rain clouds.

The sun won, and that smile changed everything.

Cameron Diaz, eat your heart out, Luke thought. Maggie Sullivan's smile was wide and infectious. She had glossed her lips some kind of soft, shimmery shade of peach, and he saw the kissable plumpness of her lower one. In the blink of an eye that smile transformed her from an old-maid schoolmarm to a woman who looked young and carefree and quite astoundingly beautiful.

Not beautiful in the Amber way, all painted and promising seduction. Beautiful in quite a different way, natural and graceful, like a doe pausing in a meadow.

He noticed the smile lit her eyes to a shade that was electric, and she had little crinkles at the edges of them that told him her smile was one hundred percent the real thing.

His eyes were drawn to the plumpness of her bottom lip again. How was it possible he had been in such close proximity to her this afternoon and not noticed how kissable her mouth was? It must be the gloss, because now it seemed he couldn't focus on anything else as she came across his nicely cleaned floor toward him.

"You're full of surprises," she said, stopping, looking up at him through a tangle of thick lashes.

Whoo boy. He was full of surprises? She was the one who was late. And here. And beautiful in some spectacular, understated way he had not appreciated in a woman before. And the biggest surprise of all? Miss Maggie had lips that could be declared dangerous weapons.

"You, too," he said.

"Me?" She laughed with disbelief and self-consciousness. "Oh, no, I don't think I'm a surprising kind of person."

"You're here," he pointed out. "That's a surprise."

"You didn't think I'd come?" The smile faded, and with it went the spell of great beauty it had cast. Not that she wasn't cute enough, if you had the librarian fantasy.

Which he didn't. Amber in black leather was all the fantasy he needed.

"No, I didn't think you'd come."

"Oh."

He noticed how awkward she was, just plain bad at the man-woman interchanges. It was a quality he should not find the least endearing.

But he did, not that it changed anything. Luke August did not date awkward girls. Or ones that were easily hurt. And yet her eyes wouldn't let him go, beckoned to him, a lighthouse to a ship lost at sea.

"So, er, why did you come? If you thought I wasn't coming?" she asked.

He lifted a shoulder. "Floor needed mopping?"

"Well, that explains the outfit."

He suddenly didn't want her thinking about his outfit for too long. He didn't want her arriving at the real reason he'd worn the disguise—to spy on her, and then to slip away, unscathed by her smile. It was too late for plan A.

Luke decided to formulate plan B as he went along. "It's part of my escape plan," he confided in her. "Nurse Nightmare takes a dim view of her patients ducking out to catch the late show."

"The late show," Maggie repeated, as if she had only just remembered why she was here. She looked around uncomfortably, took a deep breath and began talking, the fast chatter of someone who was nervous, or trying very hard to sell a product they didn't actually believe in.

"Actually, Luke," she said, "I asked you to go to the movie with me on an impulse."

"You don't say?" he said dryly.

She hurried on. "I had decided not to come. But then it seemed so unfair to leave you waiting with no explanation. So I just came to tell you, it's off. No date."

He regarded her silently. Well, well, well. Another surprise from Maggie Sullivan. She was brushing him off? It was actually much worse than just plain being stood up. He was not entirely accustomed to this turn of events. He found himself reluctantly intrigued by it, so he folded his hands more firmly over the mop, leaned his chin on the tops of his hands and let her flounder.

"You wouldn't have liked it, anyway. The movie," she added hastily as if, left to his own devices, he would have assumed *it* was something incredibly, indescribably naughty.

"Why the change of heart?" he asked, enjoying the little flood of crimson that was staining her cheeks. She had quite amazing cheekbones, when they were highlighted like that.

The voice of reason tried to interject in his inspection. *Luke,* it asked him, *when was the last time you were with a girl who blushed?*

"I just don't want to," she stammered, and then added, apparently for emphasis, "Really."

Twelve. Same age that I last took a girl to a movie.

"Really," he repeated, not quite sure if he was amused

or aggravated. "Women rarely say they don't want to. To me."

"I'm sure that's quite true, Mr. August," she said formally. Her eyes skittered away from his, looking for an escape. "I mean, it's obvious you're a very charming man. And attractive."

Her blush deepened as if telling him he was attractive was something she would now have to confess to the neighborhood priest on Saturday night.

"I have to go," she said frantically.

Not so fast, little Miss Maggie. "What part don't you want to?" he asked. He deliberately lowered his voice. He took one hand off the mop handle, tried to fight the renegade urge one more time and failed. He picked up a strand of her hair, felt the tantalizing silk of it between his thumb and finger, and then let it fall.

She gasped as if he had asked her to have sex on the foyer floor, and tucked the offended strand of hair behind her ear. "The movie part," she squeaked.

She was not in his league at all. That was evident. His league was women who knew how to play the game— who breezily returned the repartee loaded with sexual innuendo, who blinked their lashes and tossed their hair, who leaned a little closer to let him have a peek down shirts that were unbuttoned one button too low.

Luke could not have guessed it would be so much fun playing a different game, toying with Maggie. The thing was, he couldn't predict what was going to happen next with her. And that lack of predictability was just a tiny bit refreshing.

"What's so scary about a movie?" he asked, knowing darn well it wasn't the movie she was scared of.

Unless he was mistaken, little Miss Maggie found him wildly attractive. One touch of his lips on her lips, or on her neck, one little nibble on her ear, and she would probably lose control of herself.

The thought of Maggie Sullivan losing control of herself flared, white-hot, in his poor male-hormone-driven brain.

Down, Fred, he ordered himself.

"Who's Fred?" she asked, bewildered.

He realized he had spoken out loud, recovered and pointed to the name tag on the hospital-issue coveralls.

"Oh." She was very flustered.

"You were explaining about the movie," he reminded her silkily.

She looked down at her suede jacket and picked an imaginary fleck off of it. "Okay," she said, looking back at him suddenly and jutting out her chin, the determined look of a woman about to come clean, "it's about the popcorn."

"Popcorn?" he echoed. He had expected anything but that. Popcorn? Was she serious?

She nodded, deadly serious. "Do I get popcorn?"

He wondered if it was a trick question. There it was again. Every single time he thought he was sort of figuring her out, she tossed a curve at him.

"Do you want popcorn?" he asked cautiously. He was not accustomed to being with women who were complicated, hard to read, easy to offend.

"Of course! What's a movie without popcorn?"

"Agreed."

She sighed. "But if I get popcorn, then I have to decide about butter."

"That hardly seems earthshaking," he said, but he could tell she thought it was.

She sighed again, then blurted out, "Do I get my popcorn with butter the way I like it or without so that you'll think I at least try to be skinny?"

He slid his eyes over the lushness of her curves. What a shame *skinny* would be on her.

When he looked back at her face she looked earnest and indignant, and Luke found he had to put a hand up to his mouth and bite on his knuckle so he wouldn't laugh. It would be a mistake to laugh in the face of her earnestness.

"And then," she continued, "if I say to hell with what you think since you've already seen my skirt stuck around my hips—"

She didn't look like the kind of girl who used even mild curse words like *hell* very often. Dare he hope he was already being an evil influence on her?

"—and get the butter, maybe even double butter, then my fingers are covered in grease and if you try to hold my hand, not saying that you would, but—"

He held up his hand to stop the flow of words, choked down the laughter that was trying to get out and gazed down at her, trying to discern if she was attempting to amuse him or if it just came naturally to her.

It occurred to him that it had been a very long time since he'd been anything but bored with any woman, with the notable exception of Amber.

Having tamed the twitching of his lips, he finally said, "Has anybody ever suggested you might take life a tad too seriously?"

She nodded, sadly.

"I mean that is just way too much effort put into thinking about popcorn."

"I know. I'm twenty-seven years old, and I have more self-doubt than I had as a teenager. It's pathetic."

Uh-oh. If he was not mistaken, he heard a past heartbreak in there. What else took a beautiful woman's confidence from her so thoroughly? Geez. Somebody should teach this girl how to have a little fun. Not him, of course, but someone.

His voice of reason told him to wish her a polite good night and a nice life and get the hell back to his room. It told him heartbreak made women fragile. It told him he was the man least likely to be entrusted with anything fragile even for a few hours.

His voice of reason pointed out to him that she was worried about whether they were going to hold hands, for heaven's sake, and his mind was already conquering her lips and beyond.

Of course, if he was any damned good at listening to his voice of reason, he wouldn't be in the hospital for the seventh time in five years.

"What do you say we downgrade?" he suggested after a moment's thought.

"Downgrade?"

"You know, from a date. We'll just grab a cup of coffee somewhere."

She wanted to say yes. He could tell. But she didn't.

"I don't think it's a very good idea," she said uncertainly.

It was really beginning to bug him that she found him so infinitely irresistible that she was resisting with all her might.

"Why not?"

"Well, it's just the popcorn question with a different backdrop. Maybe worse. We'd have to talk. I mean just stare across the table and look at each other and think of clever things to say."

Clever? Was she kidding? You told a few blond jokes, you talked about your job and your motorcycle, you found out she'd been a cheerleader in high school and owned a poodle. Maggie expected clever? It was his turn to worry.

His voice of reason told him to bid her adieu, go back to his room and start a gratitude journal.

Entry number one could be how grateful he was to have avoided any kind of involvement with a woman who didn't know anything about flirting, dating or making small talk with the opposite sex. And also one who was so obviously a fresh survivor of a heartbreak.

"So, how do you usually get to know people?" his other voice asked. "Meaning *men* people?"

"Oh, you know. Shared interests. Work. Church."

Shared interests? Would that be the poodle or the motorbike? Work? He couldn't even picture Amber on a construction site! And the worst one of all—church?

Whoo boy, church girls were not on his list of potential dates. In his limited experience they lived by rules that all began with Thou Shalt Not. Church girls loved commitment. Made vows. Mooned over babies. Babies!

Run! His voice of reason screamed. But he wasn't running. So, he'd show little Miss Maggie Mouse, church girl, an evening of fun. Maybe he'd get himself a few points in the heaven department if he didn't encourage her to curse any more. Everybody could use a few points in the heaven department, right?

Wrong, his voice of reason said stubbornly.

It was dumb to ignore that reason-voice. Luke knew from experience you almost always ended up going off a ramp on a dirt bike at eighty miles an hour, filled with the sudden knowledge that you would have had to be going ninety to make the ramp on the far side of the ravine.

He ignored the voice of reason. This was a challenge after all. He had a weakness. He had never been able to say no to a challenge.

And he had all the scars to prove it.

"Okay, the movie is out. Coffee is out. How about if we just go down to Morgan's Pub, play a game of pool and call it a night?"

There. He'd risen to the challenge and gotten himself off the hook in one smooth move. No girl who got to know people from the church was going to say yes to going to a pub and playing pool with a virtual stranger, a renegade dressed in a custodian's outfit.

She hesitated for only a moment, filled herself up with air as if she was building up the nerve to step off a cliff into a pool of ice-cold water, and then said, "Okay. I guess that would be all right."

Maggie could not believe she had just said that. It would most definitely *not* be all right to go play a game of pool with Luke August. She didn't even know how to play pool, though that would be the least of her problems.

It was his eyes, she decided. They were green and smoky and they danced with amusement and mischief and seduction.

Seduction, she repeated to herself with a gulp.

She had come here to Portland General to tell him

politely she had come to her senses and that she was not going to a movie with a stranger, with a man she knew nothing about except that he raced wheelchairs. Badly. She could just have not come at all, but it had seemed as if it would be too rude to leave him standing there in the foyer, waiting for her.

Of course, if she was going to be honest with herself, the truth was she could have used the phone and left a message for him at the nursing station.

But then she wouldn't have known if he had come. Somehow she had thought maybe he wouldn't. What had she felt when she had first walked in and the hospital foyer had appeared empty?

Much too much.

Her resolve to break the date had intensified when Luke had touched her hair. What had she felt then? Again, much too much. As if she wanted to lean toward him, place her fingertips on his chest, feel the hard wall of muscle and man beneath her hands, as she had felt it this afternoon.

Everything in her mind was screaming at her to run. Every sinew of her body was keeping her rooted to the spot.

In the end his eyes had proved irresistible, the laughter in them beckoning to her, promising her something outside the predictability and the monotony of her own narrow world.

Look at it as homework, she persuaded herself when she heard her voice saying with deceptive calm that she would go play pool with him.

Homework assignment: *Be bold. Do something totally out of character this week.* So, she'd asked a man out. It hardly counted if she then refused to go out with him!

"My lady," Luke said, picking up the bucket and resting the dripping mop over his shoulder, "follow me."

By then she was helpless to do anything but obey. Following him allowed her to study the broadness of his back, the narrowness of his hips, the firm line of his rear end, the length of his leg.

She realized, even in those custodian's overalls, too short for his six-foot-something frame, that he walked like a man who owned the earth, his stride long and loose, powerful and confident.

"Evenin'," he said cheerfully to a nurse coming toward them.

The woman gave him a quick glance, squinted at his chest. "Evening, Fred," she replied distractedly.

Maggie stifled a giggle.

"Fred" turned and winked at her. He led her through a maze of hallways and up and down elevators until they came to an exit she suspected no one knew existed.

While she watched, he reached for the zipper on the coveralls.

"Want to take bets what I have on underneath?" His eyes were very dark in the murky light of the hall, dark and watchful.

She wished she was one of those girls who knew what to say in moments like this, but Maggie only gulped and shook her head. But she didn't look away, and he had known she would not look away.

Aware her eyes were riveted on that zipper, he lowered it very slowly, winked at her when she spotted the shirt underneath, and then he shimmied out of the coveralls, as if he undressed in front of women everyday.

Which he probably did, she reminded herself. The man was as close to irresistible as men came, and he knew it.

Underneath the coveralls, Luke had on a white denim shirt, sleeves rolled up to just below the elbow, revealing the power of his lower forearms. Faded jeans clung to the large muscles of his thighs.

"How did you know this was here?" she asked a trifle breathlessly, trying to think about anything but the way he was made.

"This exit? I explore."

"For what reason?"

"You never know when you might have to get ten old people in wheelchairs out because of a fire."

He could have said anything. That he got bored. That he was restless. And those things probably would have been true. But what he said also had sounded true. It would almost be too much to handle if he looked the way he did—so handsome, powerful, self-assured— and also had heroic qualities.

He opened the door for her and bowed. "The only one in the building that's not alarmed," he told her.

"How many alarms did you set off finding that out?" she asked, stepping by him, trying desperately to keep it light, to banter, not to give in to the shivering awareness she felt when she glimpsed the squareness of his wrist, caught the scent of him, noticed how the darkness made his faintly whisker-roughened face look like that of a pirate.

"Lots. Ask Nurse Nightmare."

"I intend to." She looked around. There was no light over the door, and it was pitch-black out here. She didn't have the foggiest notion where they were. Behind one of the hospital wings, she assumed.

He leaned over and stuck a rock in the door, holding it ajar ever so slightly. "So I can get back in."

"Why do you go to all the trouble?" she asked. "I think we could have just walked out the front door. You're a patient, not a prisoner."

"Ha. You don't know the first thing about Nurse Nightmare, do you?"

"I know her name is not Nurse Nightmare! It's Hillary Wagner."

He leaned close to her. She could feel his breath on the soft hollow of her neck. It occurred to her she was in a very dark and deserted place with a man she knew absolutely nothing about.

"I like to live dangerously," he said softly.

So, now she knew that. And yet she did not feel the least afraid, or at least not for her physical safety. When she looked into Luke August's eyes she saw a man who planned escape routes for ten people in wheelchairs and who loved to play.

And she saw something else.

Her own need. She leaned toward him, her eyes closing, her lips parting. He was leaning toward her, too, so close she could smell the tangy scent of him, feel the faint heat rising off his body. She gave in to the temptation to touch. Her fingertips grazed his shirt, and she shut her eyes against the pulsating power contained behind the thin and flimsy wall of fabric.

He pulled back, away from her touch, and she straightened and stared at him.

"Ah, Miss Maggie Mouse," he said softly, "you aren't that kind of girl."

She was grateful for the darkness because she could feel the blush leap onto her cheeks. It was true. She was not that kind of girl.

But she sure wanted to be.

"Miss Maggie Mouse?" she asked, faintly chagrined, but slightly charmed, despite herself. Boys in high school had always given the girls they liked teasing nicknames. She had never been one of those girls chosen.

"That's right," he said, his eyes warm in the darkness. "Miss Maggie Mouse."

She held her breath. She could tell he wanted to kiss Miss Maggie Mouse very badly, or at the very least, touch her hair again.

But he did neither.

He held out his hand to her, and there was no mistaking the brotherliness of the offer. She took it. His grip was strong and warm and protective. Unfortunately, he had just protected her from himself, a gesture that was completely unwanted.

"Let's go play that game of pool," he said, his voice thick.

She had a sudden, wild yearning to show him she was no mouse, to show him the mouse was only a disguise.

But for what? She wanted to be a tigress, but that was a bit of a stretch. She was a twenty-seven-year-old social worker whose one serious romance had ended like a bad Hollywood comedy.

She decided that trying to tempt Luke August might be a mistake, and yet even the notion of taking his lips captive until he was helpless with yearning filled her with a lovely, drugging warmth that was not typical of her. Even entertaining such an idea made her feel vaguely guilty.

Unaware of the war within her, Luke led them through the darkness with catlike confidence, bringing them out on a side street just to the west of the hospital.

"Morgan's is just around the corner. Have you ever been there?" he asked.

"On occasion. They have a great lunch special. Have you been there?"

He snorted. "It's where everybody knows my name."

Great, Maggie thought. He was restless and reckless. He loved to live dangerously. He was comfortable shedding his clothes in front of a woman. He was totally at home in a bar. What was she doing here?

Having the time of your life, a little voice, one she did not recognize at all, answered back to her, not without glee.

Three

Morgan's Pub was crowded. And loud. The cheerful Irish bar was a popular place in downtown Portland, and Maggie usually enjoyed the atmosphere, noise and decor, but tonight, after walking hand in hand with Luke, and after a near miss in the kissing department, it felt way too public.

Not that anyone noticed! A couple in one of the oak booths by the windows didn't seem to be even remotely aware of either the noise or the crowd. They were tangled around each other like tree roots.

Were these performances becoming more common? Or was Maggie just noticing them more?

"Sheesh," Luke muttered. "Get a room."

So, he had noticed, too. Maggie glanced once more at the couple and frowned. Wasn't that a man she had seen on several occasions at the Healthy Living Clinic?

"Hey, Luke, haven't seen you for a while."

Maggie's attention was diverted from the couple. The waitress was cute, one of those perky outgoing types that Maggie always somehow envied, even though they always seemed to end up working in places like this.

Blond and decidedly voluptuous, the girl had on a white tank top that showed off a pierced belly button. It was exactly the type of clothing that Maggie would never be able to wear. The young waitress was looking at Luke with something that seemed frighteningly close to adoration.

Maggie realized it should come as no surprise to her that Luke was the kind of man accustomed to being adored by the kind of girls who could get away with wearing skimpy white tank tops and piercing their belly buttons!

She sneaked a look at him and felt a renewed ripple of pleasure at the sheer masculine presence of the man, the dark crispness of his hair, the roguishness of his features, the rippling strength evident in every inch of his powerful frame.

A quick glance around proved his entrance had not gone unnoticed by many of the women in the establishment. A table of four attractive mid-twenties women were all looking at him with unveiled appreciation. When they caught Maggie's eye, they turned quickly away, chattering animatedly to each other over the table. Maggie suspected they were asking the very same question she herself was asking.

What was she, plain, ordinary Maggie Sullivan, doing here with this man? The movie would have been a better choice after all. She could have sat in the dark, chewed popcorn and worried about butter, never having a clue of what she was up against in terms of his massive appeal to all members of the opposite sex.

Up against? Good grief, that made it sound as if she had designs on Luke August! Maggie reminded herself she was doing her homework, being bold, not making lifetime plans. Still, she watched the interchange between Luke and the waitress with pained interest.

Luke gave the girl a light tap on the shoulder with a loose fist. "Hey, little sister," he said, and with that single phrase, seemingly tossed out casually, he defused Maggie's anxiety. The phrase recognized the girl's youth without snubbing her. He acknowledged her, but didn't encourage her interest.

Was there more to Luke than met the eye?

"Where have you been?" the waitress asked, coquettishly blinking mascara-dripping lashes at him. She slipped her tray onto her hip, apparently planning a long chat that ignored Maggie. "It's been a couple of weeks, hasn't it?"

"I've been laid up," he said. "Is there a table back in the pool room? Great. Hey, Rhonda, can you bring us a couple of burgers? Heavy on the fries. Don't stint on the gravy, either."

Maggie suspected anyone else would have been told that that wasn't her section, but Rhonda didn't seem to realize she had been gently brushed off and was still eager to please. "To drink? Your regular?"

"Yeah."

"And your lady friend?"

"Just a cola, thanks," Maggie said.

"Two regulars," Rhonda said, rolling her eyes.

Maggie and Luke pushed their way through the

crowd in the front of the bar, to the pool room at the back. There was one table to sit at, and lots of greetings to Luke. He helped her take off her jacket, the old-world courtesy completely wiped out by the wicked way he raised his eyebrows at what was underneath.

The black T-shirt was way too tight. She had known it when she put it on, but of course at that time her crystal ball had failed her. She hadn't known the evening was going to hold more than a polite refusal to see him. She had thought the jacket was staying on!

"You look great in that," he said gruffly.

The comment flustered her. Did she really? Or did he just know how to make women feel sexy?

Thankfully, they had no sooner settled at the table than he was swarmed. He fielded questions about his long absence from this favorite watering hole.

He was obviously popular and well-liked by both men and women. Though she desperately would have liked to find fault with him, Maggie found herself reluctantly liking how he interacted with people. He was a man who had been given many gifts, the kind of man who could easily have become stuck on himself.

But Luke seemed genuinely interested in other people. He knew and remembered small details. He asked one woman about her cat, and even remembered the pet's name. When he inquired about details of their lives, he appeared to care about the answers. He introduced Maggie to everyone who visited the table and made sure she was included in the conversations. He exchanged banter with some beautiful women, but never once to the point where Maggie felt he would rather be with them, or that he was asking the question she was certain everyone else was asking.

What is *he* doing with *her?*

Still, for all his comfort with the patrons of Morgan's, after a while Maggie noticed something she found a tiny bit sad, though the word *sad* seemed like the last word you would have thought of, looking at the dynamic Mr. August holding court.

"Doesn't anybody know you're in the hospital?" she finally asked when they once again had the table to themselves.

He shrugged it off. "I didn't exactly send out announcement cards."

But Maggie was a social worker. She was trained to look deeper, and her intuition was finely honed. She suspected Luke August deliberately chose relationships that were superficial, that required very little of him.

What did that say about him? Not much. It added to his already less-than-stellar résumé: that he was restless and reckless, loved to live dangerously and was quite comfortable shedding his clothes in front of women. And that was before she even began to factor in his ease at assuming roles from doctor to janitor, and his apparent love of flaunting rules.

But a more sympathetic thought was already crowding out all the unsympathetic facts. How lonely could he be that he chose relationships that asked so very little of him? That gave him nothing?

Ha! A man who looked less lonely she had rarely seen.

Besides, could it be any lonelier than her life, where she managed to bury her own heartaches in an almost crippling workload? Was escaping a life of real commitment and intimacy through overwork any different than escaping through riding motorcycles too fast or cultivating friendships in a bar?

"Hey," he said, reaching over and pressing his thumb against her forehead. "You're getting too serious, again. Tell me you are not thinking about butter."

She laughed. "No."

"Well, whatever you're thinking about, stop. You're going to get a wrinkle right here."

The small gesture, his finger briefly touching her forehead, coupled with the mischief in those green eyes, was strangely intoxicating.

Besides, he was right. The whole point of this exercise was to have fun, to let go, to be different than she normally was. Bold. She gave herself permission to do that, ordered herself to quit the analyzing that came as second nature to her, a skill that made her a great social worker but probably not such a great date.

"Is your regular drink really soda?" she asked him when their drinks arrived. "I'm surprised." Again.

"I *am* in the hospital. It's probably not a great idea to return inebriated." She realized he didn't want to discuss his less-than-macho choice of drink because he quickly changed the subject. "I can't wait for that burger. Maybe I'll have two. Hospital food is, well, horrible."

"She said it was your regular," Maggie said of his drink choice, not prepared to let him wiggle out of it.

"Did she?"

"So, unless you've been slipping out on these little field trips every night..." She already knew he hadn't, at least not to Morgan's.

"Great idea, but no. This is the first time I've had a night out. *This* hospitalization, anyway."

"*This* hospitalization?" she asked. "So you play hooky every time you're hospitalized?"

He shrugged.

"Is that a yes or a no?"

"Are you a reporter?" he teased, but did she hear a faint warning? *Don't ask too much. Don't get too personal.*

"No, I'm curious."

"You know what that did to the cat." He hesitated, then answered. "In the last five years, I've been in the hospital seven times. I get bored."

She was startled, but something in his look made her back off. She reminded herself she was supposed to be having fun. She wasn't conducting a parenting suitability interview.

"Well, here's to brown and bubbly," she said, lifting her glass to him.

"Did you have me pegged for a beer-swilling swine, little Maggie Mouse?" he teased. He liked it light. Well, that was fine. She was planning one night of being out of character. It really had nothing to do with him, except that he was a different kind of choice than she had ever made before. And how.

She ordered herself to lighten up and managed to laugh at herself. "I could picture you with a beer, yes."

"I spend too much time on motorcycles to drink much. I can't be off, even by a little bit. I don't ride with any alcohol in my system. Besides, I seem to have no problem having wrecks, even without being impaired."

So, despite the image he was trying to uphold of being a barfly, he didn't drink?

"So," she said, determined to keep it light, not to follow the tantalizing thread of all the things he didn't want her to know, like why he hung out in a bar when he didn't drink, "to you motorcycles are—"

"My life," he finished the sentence easily. "I have three. A 1994 Harley Fatboy, which is my road trip bike. Then I have an off-road bike, a Honda CRF 450, which I race. And then I have a street bike, that's kind of in pieces after, er, my last ride on it."

"What happened?"

"It's a speed bike. Sometimes irreverently called a crotch rocket. I was going a little too fast into a turn. The road was wet." He held up his glass. "Here's to leather and helmets."

He was dismissing the accident as nothing, and she reminded herself it was her night not to care, not to probe, not to try and understand, just to go with the flow, to enjoy him, to have fun.

So, a large part of his life was about motorcycles.

"I'm pretty sure I've never seen a motorcycle called a crotch rocket," she admitted. Or a Fatboy, or a CRF 450, but why admit total ignorance?

"I'll point one out to you next time we're together."

Next time they were together? She warned herself he had thrown it out casually. What were the chances there was going to be a next time?

And so, despite her vow to keep it light, Maggie wanted to know everything she could this time.

"Do you do something for a living?" she asked.

"Oh, sure. I'm in construction. All brawn, no brains."

He said that with a certain challenge, as if he expected her to disapprove.

But she could already tell there was plenty of brain there. And she had already figured out Luke did something physical. There would be no other explanation for the fine form of the man, unless he went to a gym, and somehow she couldn't envision him admiring himself in mirrors and pumping iron.

"Do you like your work?" she asked, probing the challenge she had heard in his voice.

"Love it. I was the kid who could never sit still in the classroom. Now I get paid for the fact I'm high-energy."

Should she ask him why he sounded a tiny bit defensive? No! That would be the social worker in her speaking. And tonight she was trying to be bold, different.

Instead, she said, "Not to mention the added perk that girls love muscles?"

Clearly it wasn't what he'd expected, and he tried to hide the fact she'd surprised him by saying, "Do you like muscles, Miss Maggie?"

Though she ordered them not to, her eyes immediately moved to that big, broad muscle of his exposed forearm. He flexed it.

She gulped.

He laughed and then moved easily away from her discomfort. "And how about you? What do you do for a living?"

She told him about her work at Children's Connection. Somehow she expected the same kind of disapproval that he had expected of her, or at least boredom. He did not look like the kind of guy who would list a social worker as a person of interest to him.

She could see him with a model. Spy. Airline hostess. Actress. And yet for all that, he listened to her intently, asked questions, drew her out.

It occurred to her Luke August was *great* at this. At making a woman feel special and as if she was the only one in the world. It also occurred to her it would be a mistake to take it personally, to read too much into it.

The food arrived. The hamburgers were thick and juicy, the fries homemade, the gravy sumptuous. Maggie wondered if food had ever tasted so good.

Maybe that was what being with such an intriguing man did, heightened all your senses. Wasn't that probably the point of Dr. Richie's homework assignment? Leave the comfort zone, so you could *feel* things more fully, more completely?

Before she really even knew it, she had eaten every bite of food off her plate, including a monstrous mound of French fries and every last dollop of gravy.

Luke looked at her empty plate approvingly. "You eat like a man," he said. "None of this dainty whining about getting fat."

Maggie was not at all sure that was a compliment! Didn't he remember the popcorn? She did worry about getting fat! She looked at her empty plate in horror. Oh no! Her hips had been giving her a message earlier today, and she had ignored it. Her shirt had been too tight, and she had ignored that, too!

Plus, in her frenzy over having asked Luke to go out with her, and the ensuing chaos where she had tried on everything she owned to go and tell him she *wasn't* going out with him, Maggie had completely forgotten to apply her daily dose of NoWait oil.

She shuffled through her handbag, and her hand closed over the precious little vial.

Emergency!

She excused herself and went to the washroom. She couldn't help but notice how many women were sneaking looks at Luke. Some weren't even sneaking, eyeing him up as boldly as if he were a side of prime beef and they were the supermarket meat buyer.

Despite what had seemed like very genuine interest as they had exchanged information about their jobs, he wasn't going to see anything in her. Maggie just knew it. The washroom, unfortunately, had a series of wall-to-floor mirrors and she studied herself.

Plain, she decided. And despite what Dr. Richie had said, she was not perfect. Her hips were way too wide. Her curves were just too curvy.

Reaching into her bag, she took out the NoWait. Half the recommended dose?

"Forget that, Dr. Richie," she muttered to herself.

Maggie rubbed the full dose behind her ears, and then just for good measure added another little dab.

"Goodbye, burger," she said.

She reentered the pool room, stood in the archway, and watched Luke for a moment. He was so sure of himself. The fact that he was still alone surprised her—and didn't seem to bother him one little bit. Looking at him, she felt as if he was taking her breath away.

Maggie was not sure she had ever had such a physical awareness of a man as she had of Luke. Was it because of their first encounter? Because she had felt the solidness of him against her, felt his warmth and his fire on much too intimate terms?

Was it because he had, however unintentionally, introduced her to her own yearning? For a moment, she thought of bolting for the door. Dealing with this unfamiliar territory felt the same as navigating a minefield.

But then Luke noticed her and, grinning as though he was thrilled to see her, waved her back over to him.

"So, are you ready for some pool? I got us one of the tables."

"Sure," she said doubtfully.

But half an hour later Maggie was giggling helplessly as she leaned over the table trying to hit the white ball into one of the solid ones.

"No, no, no," he said sternly. "You have to get down farther. You have to be looking right down the shaft of the cue."

He came up behind her and fitted his body around hers, adjusting her over the cue. He took her arm.

"Relax. Your elbow has to be loose. Loose! You feel like you have your arm in a splint from elbow to wrist. Geez, you smell good."

That was the contradiction. Relax? With the most gorgeous, sexy man in the universe draped around her? All the places where his body touched hers were tingling. She wanted to drop the pool cue and flip over, so that he had her bent over the pool table and she could feel the hard length of him, just the way she had on the foyer floor this morning.

She reminded herself she had condemned that man and woman on the hospital's front steps for their public display of affection....

"I'm losing my mind," she muttered.

"Concentrate!"

Sure. The question was on what? He had said she smelled good. That was the NoWait with its pleasant citrus fragrance, underlaid ever so subtly with a hint of musk.

But his smell was intoxicating, and she was pretty sure he wasn't wearing any scent except the one that came off his skin, clean, faintly tangy and perturbingly masculine.

"Okay," he said, his breath stirring the hair on the nape of her neck. "Bring your arm back." Lightly he guided her arm back, his fingers on her elbow.

"You're tickling me!"

"For God's sake, woman, concentrate. Loose elbow. Tap the cue ball. Ticklish, hmm? I'm filing that away for future reference."

There he was mentioning the future again!

Maggie hit the cue ball with all the pent-up frustration that had built within her breast, and it responded by promptly jumping over the ball she was aiming at. It flew off the table and rolled across the floor underneath the neighboring table.

Luke undraped his body from around hers, folded his arms over his chest and gave her a stern look. "What does the word *tap* mean to you?"

She straightened from where she had been bent over the table, and turned to face him.

Gazing up into the unblinking green of his sparkling eyes, she noticed how thick his lashes were, as if they had been dipped in India ink. Her mind went completely blank. "Tap? Water faucet?"

He groaned.

"I've never been athletic, Luke. It's hopeless." That was exactly how she felt. Hopeless. Hopelessly, helplessly, impossibly attracted to him.

"Athletic? You have to be an athlete to play baseball. To ski. To run foot races. Playing pool does not require athleticism."

"If it requires hand-to-eye coordination, it's hopeless," she told him. Gosh, he looked cute, bristling with that kind of mock irritation, his eyes narrowed on her. His beard had darkened with the late hour. It looked as if it would scratch in the most delightful way.

It occurred to her she wanted to kiss him. Madly. Wildly. And that she didn't care who was watching.

The thought was so uncharacteristic that she glanced at her drink. It was just cola, wasn't it?

"It's math, pure and simple," he informed her. "You figure the angle. You apply the correct amount of pressure. You have to know the difference between a tap and a slam. It's that easy."

The surge of passion that was affecting her was apparently having no effect on him at all. If it was, he wouldn't be talking so casually about taps and slams.

Not that either of those words had ever had an erotic meaning to her before. She looked at his lips, the gorgeous green of his eyes, the pulse that beat steady and strong in the hollow of his throat and felt almost dizzy.

My God, she thought, *I'm swooning.*

Maggie knew it was impossible. She was not the type of girl who swooned, of all things. She was reliable. She was pragmatic. She was responsible. Passion, and all the recklessness it implied, was for other people.

"Are you okay?"

He was suddenly right in front of her, looking down, his eyes surveying her face with concern. He took her shoulders firmly between his hands. "Maggie!"

"I'm sorry. I—" She gave up and leaned into him.

"Fresh air," he said. He bustled her through the crowd, putting people none-too-gently out of his way.

Moments later, they were standing outside the front doors of Morgan's, the laughter and noise now muted in the background. Maggie took in several deep gulps of the cool, night-scented air. His arm stayed around her shoulder, protective, surprisingly tender.

"I'm sorry," she said, truly embarrassed. "I don't know what came over me."

"You looked like you were going to faint," he said, studying her carefully. "The color is starting to come back into your cheeks now."

"I've never fainted in my whole life," she protested, but weakly. The night air was just what she needed. She could feel herself coming to her senses. His scent did not seem quite so overpowering. She avoided looking at him and moved away from under the weight of his arm, though it took a great deal of effort to get her feet to obey her command to move away from him.

"I should get back to the hospital, anyway," he said, consulting his watch. "I'll just go back and settle the bill and grab your jacket. Two seconds. Don't move. And breathe."

When he returned, he helped her into her jacket. He was going to take her hand, but she quickly inserted both hands into her coat pockets. He noticed the deliberate action with a quizzical raise of his eyebrows, but she pretended she didn't care.

The truth was she was frightened. Maggie Sullivan did not lose control.

She could not subject herself to any more temptation

tonight. Not when she felt so uncertain about how she would react to it.

They walked back to the hospital in silence. He whistled under his breath, a happy little song that only served to remind her that the strength of what she had just experienced at the pool table in Morgan's had been completely one-sided.

"I'll walk you to your car," he said when they came to the hospital lot, "and then I'll slip in the side door where we came out. I don't want you over there by yourself at this time of night."

It wasn't until he said that, that Maggie realized she had been anticipating going back to that spot, cloaked in darkness and utter privacy.

"Thank you," she said, hearing the stiffness in her own voice, and ducked from the query in his eyes. She fished through her bag for her keys when they arrived at her car, a new gold Volkswagen Beetle.

"Cute," he said. "Just about what I would have figured."

"Really?"

"I like to do that. Figure out what people drive. It tells me about them."

"What does my car tell you?"

"Cute," he repeated.

"I have to go," she said hastily. "It was fun, Luke, really it was."

"Hey."

His hand on her upper arm stopped her from flinging herself into the car and making her escape.

"What's wrong?" he asked.

Oh, Luke. Don't do this. Don't be sensitive, on top of being gorgeous and charming and a man I can't have.

"Nothing."

"Something changed back there in the pool room. Did I say something? Did I hurt you?"

"No, of course not."

"Because I can do that. Without meaning to. Beak off and not even realize I'm stepping on people's feelings."

"You didn't step on my feelings."

And then the self-control she had been trying so hard to exercise snapped. She turned full to him, let go of her grip on the car's door handle. She twined her arms around the strong, beautiful column of his neck, and she stood on tiptoe.

And she kissed him. It wasn't the kiss of Little Miss Mouse, either. No, the tigress was unleashed.

At first, he went very still. And then he pressed himself hard against her, and his hands went to the small of her back and pulled her even closer into him, so close she could feel his heat, and it fueled the fire that was raging within her.

Out of control.

Miss Maggie Mouse was totally out of control. And loving it. His hands moved from the small of her back to tangle in her hair, to bring her lips in fuller contact with his.

Flashpoint. Maggie was on fire. Heat, glorious and sizzling, enveloped her entire being. She could feel her bones melting, her skin, as her body met the hard line of his.

His lips, which had looked so firm, were deliciously soft under hers, and yet no less commanding.

He was hungry for more than a break from hospital food. That became evident very, very quickly. He plundered her mouth, his kiss hot and destructive and glorious, like slowly rolling lava. When she felt he would ignite her, as if the fire of his kiss would consume her and leave nothing behind but smoldering ash, he lifted his lips from hers. He spread small kisses from her neck to her earlobes, hot spots of delight so intense it was painful. He tormented her eyelids, and her cheeks, and the tip of her nose. She had been right about his whiskers. The scrape of them across the soft flesh of her cheek was heady. Then his lips returned to her mouth again.

She was totally unaware of anything but him, lost in the passion of the moment, swimming in the fire, headily and completely consumed by it, her senses blocking out everything but him. The way he tasted and smelled and felt.

The way he tasted and smelled and felt affected her, making her feel alive.

She had been unaware that she was dead, but now she was like a sleeping princess brought to life by the touch of his lips.

He yanked away from her.

"Someone's coming," he said in an undertone.

How had he noticed that? She had noticed nothing. No better than that woman on the steps of the hospital earlier today, or that man at the booth in Morgan's.

She peered past Luke, saw the white jacket of a doctor coming off duty. It was someone she'd worked with occasionally in conjunction with her cases at Children's Connection.

He saw her, recognized her, and his eyebrows shot up.

Furious embarrassment rushed through her body, heated and ugly.

Maggie broke away from Luke. She grasped for her car door again. "I don't know what came over me," she said. "Sorry."

"Sorry?" Luke said. "Are you crazy?"

"Apparently." She slid into her car, using all the discipline she could muster. She couldn't look at him again.

But she did.

He stood there under the dim light of the parking lot streetlamp. He was big and self-assured, all barely contained masculine grace and power. In a nutshell Luke August was way more man than she would ever be able to handle.

Never again did she want to unleash whatever had been unleashed inside her tonight. It was too strong a drug.

She ordered herself to drive away. She even started the engine. But Luke still stood there, his hands in his pockets, looking at her.

What was that expression?

He was stunned, obviously. By her performance. By how out of control she had been. Well, that made two of them.

But there was something more there in his expression that she could not read.

She could not explain to him what had happened just now. She could not say, *I am not that kind of woman,* when she had just been exactly that kind of woman. Instead, she rolled down her window, just a crack.

"It would be best if we didn't see each other again," she said.

He looked at her steadily, then nodded. "I think you're right," he agreed.

She drove away quickly, before he had a chance to see how much his quick agreement had hurt her.

Luke folded his arms over his chest and watched Maggie leave the parking lot. Somehow he had not figured her for the kind of gal who would squeal her tires.

But then what had he figured right about her so far?

The answer was nothing. He just was not reading her right. That kiss! He was still smoking from the heat of it.

And trembling slightly, if he was going to be totally honest about it.

The truth was that was the way he had always imagined Amber would kiss—with a kind of no-holds-barred intensity that left a man feeling as though the world was disappearing, crumbling beneath his feet.

As if there was nothing that remained but sweet, soft lips, and hot, lush curves pressed into his chest.

Wait! If he looked the world over he would never find a woman less like Amber than little Miss Maggie Mouse.

Amber would drive a vintage fire-engine-red Barracuda convertible. Amber would wear short leather skirts and sashay her hips. She would hustle pool, not flub balls onto the floor. She would drink whiskey not soda.

All in all Amber was not the kind of girl a boy took home to Mama.

Which was the whole idea. Luke August had decided a long, long time ago he was never taking a girl home to Mama.

Or at least not one Mama would approve of.

And he had a feeling his mother would approve of Maggie. Maggie with her soft eyes, and her obvious intelligence and decency. Maggie who helped little children as her life's work, and didn't have a clue how sexy she was.

He would have had never to see her again for that reason alone, even if she had not suggested it first.

Though, going back to his room he had to admit that he was just a tiny bit frosted that Maggie had mentioned it first.

She must have been a whole lot less shaken by that kiss than he had been.

In the maintenance closet, he carefully returned Fred's stuff to where it had been. He stuck five bucks in the pocket so Fred could have a coffee on him in exchange for the loan he didn't know he had made.

Luke donned his gown over his jeans and sidled down the hall.

"Mr. August! Where have you been? Evening meds were over an hour ago."

He turned to look at the night nurse. "Oh, just down in the TV room."

"I looked there for you."

"I went to the TV lounge on the next floor. They were tuned into something a little too tender on this one. One of those bachelorette things where she gives some poor sucker a rose. You know. Gigantic yuck."

"Um-hmm."

The nurse was older and had on sensible shoes and her uniform was pressed with military precision, but her face was kind and she was not at all like Nurse Nightmare.

"You don't believe me?" he asked, all innocence and wonder.

She leaned close to him.

"You have lipstick on your neck. Glossy. Peach-colored."

"Oh." Damn her observation skills. Luke had not wanted to think about glossy peach-colored lips again tonight. Or ever.

"Get to your room before I report you."

"Yes, ma'am."

"Did you have fun?" she asked as he headed down the hall.

"I'm still trying to figure that out," he muttered, as much to himself as to her.

Four

Luke woke up in a nasty mood. That rarely happened to him. He nearly always woke up full of plans for his day, with a song in his heart—usually "What Do You Do With a Drunken Sailor?"—which he happily and loudly shared with anybody within earshot.

But this morning he gloomily contemplated the pure white of his hospital-room ceiling. He felt crabby and out of sorts. It had, he decided firmly, nothing at all to do with Maggie Mouse telling him she never wanted to see him again.

Not that the name Maggie Mouse was going to do now that he knew the stunning truth. The girl kissed like a house on fire.

He'd have to come up with a new name for her. If he was ever going to see her again, which he wasn't.

"So, no problem," he said out loud. The real problem was this place. It was time to get out of here. He had way too much time on his hands, way too much time to think.

But when the doctor came on rounds, she did not look impressed to see him in his street clothes, his bag packed.

"No," she said sternly, when he announced his plans for the day. "If I let you out of here, you would go straight back to work, the same as you did last time."

"What if I promise?" he asked.

"You promised last time!"

"But last time I had my fingers crossed." He held out his hands in front of him, a gesture of sincerity and honesty that she was not the least taken in by.

"Your body needs more time to repair itself." She carefully explained to him what the most recent injuries to his back would do if he stressed them too soon. She mentioned words like *permanent disability* and *wheelchair,* which of course he knew to be baloney.

He was as strong as a team of oxen.

"I don't think I can stay, Doc. I'm going out of my mind. The food stinks, and there's nothing to do." What he didn't say was that he did not need time to think about Maggie Sullivan or that kiss or how much fun he'd had playing pool with her or the way that black T-shirt had molded around her luscious curves.

Or her final words to him.

But even though he didn't elaborate, the good doc seemed to get it, that with or without her approval he was on short time now.

"All right," she agreed with a sigh, "I'll read the report from your physiotherapy session today, and if it's good, we'll talk about this some more tomorrow."

"I'm leaving tomorrow," he said.

"Your insurance won't cover any of this unless I sign for your discharge."

He gave her his high-voltage smile. She tried to look stern, but he could tell she couldn't resist that smile. "Which you will, right?"

"I said we'd talk about it tomorrow."

But he knew it was settled. There. He was getting some control back over his life. He felt a little glimmer of his normal cheerfulness. By the time he'd ordered breakfast from the fast-food joint around the corner, enough for the whole ward, and had it delivered to the hospital, he was in a pretty good mood, passing out hash browns and egg sandwiches while serenading the other patients with "What Do You Do With a Drunken Sailor?"

"Mr. August!"

He had stopped to chat with a young nurse between rooms and deliveries, and he turned to see Nurse Nightmare bearing down on him. Out of the corner of his eye, he saw the young nurse disappear.

He braced himself.

"Have you seen Billy yet this morning?"

"No, ma'am. I was going to bring him breakfast, though."

She glanced at the brown paper bag, and he waited for the disapproving lecture. But it didn't come.

"He's not himself," she said in a low voice. "I was hoping you might cheer him up. Without wheelchair racing, of course."

"He's sick?" Luke asked, and felt the fist of fear close around his heart. He'd been right. It was time to get out of here. There were too many sick people around. You didn't want to go getting attached to sick people.

She shook her head. "Not any sicker than usual. He's sad, Mr. August."

Sad. Sheesh. A sad seventeen-year-old boy with cancer. What Luke wanted to do was run the other way. He had nothing to offer in a situation like this. Nothing. He was rough and gruff, an unpolished construction crew boss.

"I wouldn't know what to do for him," he said. "I'm not great in the sensitivity department."

"Look, you self-centered lunkhead," the nurse said. "Require more of yourself!"

She marched away, leaving him to stare after her, oddly hurt, though working in his field he'd been called worse and told off better many, many times.

"Self-centered lunkhead," he repeated to himself. He was delivering breakfast to the other inmates. Didn't that count?

No longer singing, he finished his deliveries, annoyed that Nurse Nightmare had managed to get under his skin. So, if he did require more of himself, what would he do for Billy to cheer him up? Order a cake that a girl jumped out of? Pretend to be Patch Adams?

The truth was, he didn't have a clue, and the more he thought about Billy being sad, the more he wished he could be the one to help, to change it, to fix it. Maybe he didn't have a clue what to do, but he knew someone who did. He thought of the softness of her big hazel eyes. He reminded himself they weren't going to see each other again.

But this was an emergency!

He looked at the clock, then went down to the phone at the end of the hall and looked up the Children's Connection phone number.

His heart seemed to be beating way too fast as he waited to be put through.

"Maggie Sullivan."

She certainly sounded chipper this morning! Why had he assumed she would be as gloomy as he was?

"Maggie Sullivan," she said again.

"Hi, Maggie."

There was a long silence, and then she said his name.

He was not sure his name had ever sounded like that before. A breath, a whisper, a prayer.

He wanted to ask her how she felt. How she had slept. If she had thought of him the first thing when she woke up.

But it would be like signing a confession saying how he felt, how he had slept, what he had thought of first thing upon waking.

"Um, Maggie, I have this little problem. I was hoping you could help me with it." As he explained the situation, he tried to think when the last time was that he had ever asked anyone for help with a problem. It had been a long, long time ago.

He realized, suddenly, and not with good grace, that something had lived within him, ignored and unidentified until this very moment.

Loneliness.

"So," she repeated back to him what he had just told

her, "Billy's feeling sad this morning, and Hillary thought you could help?"

"That's right. But I can't, Maggie. I don't know what to say. I'm good at joking around. Small talk." He decided not to tell her his idea about the girl jumping out of the cake. "Can you help me?"

"Do you want me to come?"

The question was posed softly, and yet he felt as if he was a man who had been trapped in the chilly depths of an icy crevasse, who had resigned himself to his fate, and then was suddenly thrown a rope.

He marveled that last night she had told him so firmly she could not see him again, and yet she put that aside instantly when the welfare of a child she didn't even know was at risk.

"Yeah," he said after a moment. "I want you to come."

"I'll be there in fifteen minutes. I'll meet you at the nurses' station."

"Thanks, Maggie."

He hung up the phone and stared at it. He had just called a woman he barely knew and asked her to help him. A woman who had said in no uncertain terms she never wanted to see him again. He should not feel good about that at all.

But he felt okay. He hummed his favorite ditty.

She arrived in ten minutes, five minutes early, precisely the kind of woman he had pegged her for before their "date" last night.

She looked like who she really was today, too. Her lustrous hair was coiled in a neat bun, she had on a slack suit in an uninspiring color that reminded him of porridge. She even had a little pair of granny glasses perched on her nose.

And underneath that was a secret they shared. A kiss that made that outfit such a lie.

He tried to keep that kiss out of his mind as he strolled toward her. He suspected she did, too.

"Thanks for coming." He felt as if he was looking beyond the glasses to the richness of her eyes. He could imagine the hair spinning down over her shoulders, wondered what kind of underwear she had on.

It occurred to him it might have been a mistake to call her.

But that feeling didn't last. In a few moments, he knew she had been exactly the right person to call.

They went together into Billy's room. He was lying with his back to the door and them, looking very small and fragile under the blanket.

"Hi, Billy," he said.

"I don't feel like racing wheelchairs today, Luke."

"That's okay. I don't either. I brought you some breakfast."

"Thanks." But Billy did not turn toward them.

"I wanted to introduce you to a friend of mine," Luke said.

Billy turned, the whole cocoon of his blanket turning with him.

Maggie went forward and put out her hand, forcing him to emerge from under the blanket to take it.

"I'm Maggie Sullivan."

"Billy Harmon."

She pulled up a chair and sat down, leaning forward, her hand cupped under her chin. "This is a lousy place to spend a gorgeous July day," she said.

"I have cancer," Billy said without preamble.

Luke tried to think whether Billy had ever told him he had cancer. He didn't think so. It had been one of the nurses or Billy's parents who had told him.

"What kind?" she asked softly, her voice soothing.

The floodgates opened. Billy told her what kind, and how long he'd been fighting it. Luke was astounded to know this poor kid had been in and out of the hospital since he was twelve years old. He'd lost all his hair. His friends treated him differently. His mom cried all the time.

And Luke had been wheelchair racing with him?

Then the boy was crying. Big racking sobs that Luke could feel inside his own body. He eyed the door, but he could see Maggie being so brave. She took the boy's hand.

He eyed the door once more, heard Nurse Nightmare in his mind telling him to require more of himself, and he went to the other side of the bed. He took Billy's other hand.

"Luke, I don't want you to see me crying," Billy choked. "Guys like you don't cry, do they?"

He thought of his life. Had he deliberately made it into an emotional wasteland, where there were no tears because there was absolutely nothing worth crying about? "Hey. Everybody cries."

"Do you?"

He felt as close to it at the moment as he had felt for years, so it was no lie when he said, "Yeah."

"When?"

Hell. But he suddenly remembered something. "When I was about your age I had a dog. My mom hated her. Said she made our house smell bad, and that there was dog hair on the furniture. One day I came home from school, and no more Stinkbomb."

"You named your dog Stinkbomb?" Billy asked, and the first wisp of a grin flitted across his face.

This was more like it! "And for obvious reasons," Luke said. "That dog could—" He suddenly remembered Maggie. "Uh, let's just say the dog was an impressive performer in the stink department."

"So, your Mom was right?" Maggie asked. "The dog made the house smell bad?"

Luke frowned. He had never once in his life considered the possibility that his mother might have been right about anything. Had the dog really made life that uncomfortable for other people?

The problem with a girl like Maggie was she might make you look at your whole life from a different, deeper, more mature perspective. And who wanted to do that?

"You cried when Stinkbomb went missing?" Billy asked.

"Like a baby." He didn't add that then he'd gone out on a stolen motorbike and had his first extremely impressive wreck. He'd broken his leg in four places.

But the admission that Luke had a softer side seemed to ease something in Billy. He looked at him for a long time, sighed, and then looked away.

"I just feel so scared," Billy said. "I think I'm going to die."

Every problem Luke had ever faced suddenly seemed small and insignificant. It seemed like there was nothing meaner in the world than a seventeen-year-old boy facing that kind of fear, a fear no one could help him with, no matter what they said or did.

He wanted to say with false confidence, "Of course you aren't going to die," but he didn't know if it was true, and Maggie caught his eye suddenly, as if she had guessed what he wanted to say. She gave a slight shake of her head.

"Is there something you would do if you were going to die?" she asked softly.

Billy wiped the tears from his face and nodded solemnly. "I'd make a will. When I try to tell my mom what I want, she goes off the deep end. It's just little stuff, like to give my kid brother my goldfish and my baseball glove, and to put my paper route money in my sister's college account."

"I don't think those are little things," Maggie said softly. "Not at all."

Luke didn't, either. The kid was thinking of his own death, and he wasn't thinking of himself—the things he had left to do, the places he wanted to see—he was thinking of the people who loved him.

Luke had another aching feeling that his own life was a wasteland.

"I'd like them to play 'Amazing Grace' on the bagpipes at the funeral." Billy smiled wryly. "Not a single soul, besides you two, even knows I like the bagpipes."

Luke decided Maggie was the bravest damn woman in the world, because she didn't flinch from any of that. He was mulling over the discovery that Billy had a brother and sister, and clenching and unclenching his fists behind his back, trying to keep himself from giving in to the emotion that clawed at his throat.

Maggie nodded thoughtfully. "Do you want to write it down and give it to me for safekeeping? Then if the time does come, I'll know and I'll look after it for you."

Luke felt the depth of her courage, and he saw in

Billy's face a truth about Maggie that was worth more than gold. She was a woman a person could trust.

Billy nodded, relief apparent in the lines of his young face. Amazingly, he seemed happier than when they had walked in. "I'll do that today. I'm going to start right away. Thanks, Maggie. See you later, Luke."

In the hall, Luke gazed down at Maggie, seeing her in a new light. She was rich and deep and any guy who had named his dog Stinkbomb was probably completely unworthy of her. "What you did in there was great. Thanks."

"I was glad to help out, Luke."

"How did you know what to say?"

"I didn't, really. I just paid attention to my intuition."

She looked at her watch, gave a little yelp of dismay and moved away rapidly, waving over her shoulder. "I'm late! Bye, Luke."

So nothing was changed. She still thought it was best they didn't see each other. Well, maybe she was right. She was the one with the intuition.

Because he had seen things in her eyes in that room that made him understand he was completely unworthy of her. Still, watching her move rapidly away, he wished it could be different.

But then, glancing back at Billy's room, didn't he wish all of life could be different?

Maggie decided it had been a dumb thing to answer Luke's call for help. Not that she regretted helping Billy. In fact, she intended to look in on the boy as often as she could. Catastrophically ill children had special challenges, including feeling guilty about the stress their illness was causing others. So guilty, that they were alone with all their worst fears. She could help Billy with that, and wanted to.

But Luke… He was a different question.

She had awoken this morning with his kiss still searing her lips, a strange and wonderful song singing within her.

Despite the fact she had announced she was never going to see him again, she had felt a delicious sense of well-being this morning.

But wasn't that why she was taking the Bold and Beautiful seminar? To unlock her capacity for happiness, to move closer to having a fulfilling life? There was another B&B seminar this afternoon, and maybe that was why she had awakened this morning feeling happy and adventurous. Of course, she doubted that was the true reason, a doubt that had been confirmed when Luke called.

Then those lovely tingling feelings had escalated to something near delirium when she had recognized the sexy growl of his voice on the other end of her phone.

It was really what she had least expected. And what did it mean that he had called her about Billy?

That he trusted her, for one.

Trust was a lovely thing, of course, but a long way from what she was feeling for Luke. She had felt it again as soon as she had seen him strolling down the hospital corridor toward her, looking big and buff and self-assured.

That swooning feeling had come over her again, milder than before, thank heavens. And she had been able to block out his presence, for the most part, when she'd talked to Billy.

But afterward she had felt a familiar sensation of weakness, of wanting, and she had practically run away from him on some feeble excuse.

Now, hours later as she sat in her office, Luke August was still the strongest thing on her mind. Obviously, the decision not to see him again had been the right one, given the effect he had on her. But as the day passed, she became less certain in her conviction that she had done the right thing.

Maybe something she learned at the seminar this afternoon would help her know what to do next.

Her secretary came in and studied her thoughtfully.

"Are you okay today, Maggie?"

"Of course. What makes you ask?"

"You kind of have this goofy look on your face."

"I do?"

"A little funny half smile, as if you know a secret."

"Nonsense," she said, wiping any vestiges of a smile from her face.

"And who is Luke?"

"Pardon?" she said on a gasp.

The secretary, Joy, passed her some papers she had worked on that morning. In each space where she should have written a name on a contract, only the surname was correct.

The first name she had inserted was Luke!

"Isn't that silly?" she muttered, grabbing back the papers. "I'll redo these tomorrow."

Joy smiled at her. "I shouldn't have said you look goofy. You actually look nice. Kind of radiant. The way my cousin looked for a year or so after she got married. Have you met a guy, then?"

Maggie stammered but Joy gave her no time to reply.

"I hope you have. Nobody in this whole office ever knew what you saw in Mr. Booths, believe me. And just for the record, you didn't deserve what he did to you, but you were darned lucky he did do it to you. Imagine being married to *him*."

She shut the door and left Maggie sitting there with her cheeks burning. No one had ever really discussed her relationship with Darnel Booths.

Or at least not in front of her.

He had been a fellow social worker. A nice guy, devoted to his work, not spectacular in any way. Maggie had been attracted to the fact he was solid and reliable. They had dated and somehow evolved into a couple. When he had asked her to marry him, she had been so excited. Planning the wedding had been so much fun.

He had not shown up at the church.

There she had stood in her long white dress waiting, along with four bridesmaids, a flower girl, a ring bearer, a best man, a hundred and three guests and a minister.

Sometimes she wondered how she had survived the embarrassment, the humiliation. Sometimes she knew she had not survived, not completely.

For a part of her had died. She had chosen Darnel partially because he had seemed like the safest of men. Predictable and ordinary, just like her.

He had called her from Mexico that night, filled with remorse, not sure what had happened. The church had been a left turn, and he had made a right. He'd gone to the airport and used one of their honeymoon tickets, boarded the flight they were supposed to be on together to the Mayan Riviera. It was cold feet with a vengeance.

He was sorry. He could never make it up to her. And no, he did not want her to join him, and no, he wasn't coming back.

From time to time she got postcards from her "predictable and ordinary man" from the snorkeling school he was now employed at in Manzanillo, Mexico. He was sorry. He was happy. He was sorry he was happy.

In retrospect, it had been a blessing. She realized now she had been more excited about planning the wedding—her perfect fairy-tale day—than she had ever been about Darnel.

The whole fiasco had been more than three years ago. Time to get over it. But somehow she knew you never quite got over something like that.

And if you couldn't trust a man like Darnel, it begged the question whom you could trust.

Luke August? That seemed unlikely. She was acting like a love-struck teen and she knew it. Doodling his name all over official documents.

Even thinking of him now and trying to fight her thoughts, only seemed to intensify them. She should seek him out, without his knowing, just look at him, study him in the light of what Darnel had done to her. That should help her take away the larger-than-life image she was carrying around.

That was what she'd do. She'd take a casual walk through his ward on her way to the Bold and Beautiful seminar.

Gathering up her purse, she said goodbye to Joy, her heart hammering in her throat as if she was being sent on a spy mission into deepest, darkest Afghanistan.

On his ward she found out through some cloak-and-dagger work that would have done him proud, that Luke was at a physiotherapy session.

It was a perfect setup. The physio room had mirror windows into the hallway. Maggie stood there and watched.

She tried to think of Darnel.

But she could not hold the thought of Luke and another man in her mind at the same time.

Luke was dressed in a muscle shirt and shorts. His skin was absolutely gorgeous, copper silk stretched taut over well-formed muscle.

At the instructions of his therapist he was doing chin lifts on a bar.

"We've got to build the strength in your upper back before we can send you back to work. And you're not going back to work until you can pump out twenty-five of those." Maggie listened as he was given instructions, her eyes glued on him.

His face was set in fierce lines of concentration.

She counted with him, fascinated by the play of muscle. The first few chin lifts went smoothly, almost effortlessly, not even his facial expression changing.

Then she could tell he was having to dig in, to find a little more. His brow furrowed, a sheen of fine sweat appeared on that glorious skin. His muscles corded and contracted and bunched in an amazingly masculine ballet.

At fifteen, pain entered the picture. She could see him turning inward, trying to find the place within him where a reserve of strength remained.

His eyes were closed now. His limbs were trembling. His mouth was a formidable line of pain and determination. He was like an Olympic athlete training for his event.

It was obvious to her he was way past the limits of his strength, that his injury caused him pain, and yet he was not giving up and not letting go.

"That's enough," the therapist said, at eighteen. "We'll try it again tomorrow."

Luke's arms were trembling. He couldn't have one more left in him. And yet she could see him gathering himself mentally.

And then he gave a shout, pure and primal and strong. And lifted his chin up over that bar, not once more but seven more times in rapid succession.

He let go of the bar and collapsed, arms braced on his knees, sweat pouring off him, his expression calm and determined and exhausted.

"If I can impress you," she heard him tell the therapist, "the doctor is letting me out of here."

"Don't worry. You've impressed me. With your utter stupidity. You're in here to repair those injuries, not to strain them."

Luke's expression remained calm, the tirade washing over him, but not touching him. He turned his head to grab a towel and wipe his brow on it.

Maggie leaped back into the shadows. Had he seen her?

She suddenly felt embarrassed. She was like a high-school girl spying on the boys' team. Of course, she'd never done that in high school, and she suddenly regretted it.

It was a delicious guilty little pleasure. Worth the risk, she decided. Because Luke liked to play it as if he was light and lively and just a barrel of laughs. As if he was full of mischief and kisses, and nothing of substance was there.

But this morning in Billy's room she had caught a look at Luke's substance. And now she had seen it again. At the core of the man were strength and depth and determination in breathtaking abundance.

She hurried away before anyone else caught sight of her. It had been fun looking at him without it having to go anywhere. It had been like getting a fix.

But what was she going to do once he left the hospital?

She didn't want to think about it. She hurried off to her seminar.

It wasn't like her to be late, and her friend Kristen gave her a quizzical look when she slipped in the back door and took the seat Kristen had saved for her.

"What on earth have you been doing?" Kristen hissed.

"What do you mean?" she whispered back.

"You look like the cat who stole the cream."

"I do not."

"No, you're right. You look more like a woman who has had a wild and very naughty adventure."

"I do?"

"Give," Kristen said, eyeing her.

"I was just doing my homework from last time."

"We had homework?" Kristen whispered.

"Be bold. Do something totally out of character this week."

"Really?"

The lady in front of them turned and gave them a murderous look for chatting during Dr. Richie's presentation.

"Coffee break. I want the goods," Kristen said out of the side of her mouth.

Considering how much she had been looking forward to this seminar, Maggie found she was having difficulty concentrating. She looked around. Sure enough, there was the man she'd seen in Morgan's last night, and there was the woman she'd seen on the front steps of the hospital.

Both of them were beaming ridiculously.

Maggie could only assume they were as satisfied with their homework as she was. She focused on Dr. Richie. He was such an appealing man. His speaking style was so warm and enthusiastic. He seemed wise and appealing and as if, for a relatively young man, he understood so much about life.

Still, even feeling as she did about him, her attention wandered.

"I want just to leave you with this preview of your homework before you go to coffee," he said, and his words penetrated her daydream.

"Go after what you want. Erase self-doubt."

It felt as though the words were spoken only to her. And Maggie knew exactly what she wanted, and exactly what was holding her back from it.

Self-doubt. How could Dr. Richie have known that?

She thought of that dress she had been eyeing up in Classy Lass. What had stopped her from buying it? Self-doubt.

She doubted that she was the kind of woman who could pull off a sexy dress like that. She doubted that she would have a place to wear it, or a person to wear it for.

But in the last twenty-four hours, all that had changed.

"I have to go," she told Kristen, getting up and sidling past the knees of all the people still seated.

"Go where?" Kristen asked, flabbergasted.

"I just remembered something I have to do." She hurried out the doors of the Healthy Living Clinic. What if the dress wasn't there anymore?

"I'll take it as a sign," she told herself. And then she laughed out loud. "No, I won't. I'll find an even better one."

Carrie Martin sat at the back of the seminar when they came back in from coffee. She looked around the room, trying to mask her cynicism, trying to mask how appalled she was at the gullibility of these people. Couldn't they see right through "Dr. Richie"?

She was willing to bet he hated being called that. He probably tolerated it because that popular TV doctor, so successful, allowed people to call him by his first name.

She did nothing to draw attention to herself, but she knew he would never recognize her. Everything about her had changed in twenty years.

Her hair color, her eye color. She was fifty pounds lighter than the pudgy girl who had married Richard Strokudnowski right out of high school. They'd been small-town kids from Apopka, Florida. Only, Richard had harbored big-time dreams.

She had wanted the things women of that age had wanted: a little bungalow with a white picket fence, babies, a swing set and a blow-up wading pool. Carrie had dreamed small, lovely dreams.

Richard had dreamed of glory.

Back then hadn't she been just like these people? Richard had a certain charm, there was no denying it. And he'd had years to perfect it. Once, she had looked at him with the same starry-eyed gaze that he was now eliciting from the loyal following here.

"I'd like to hear some NoWait success stories to kick off our second half," her ex-husband said suavely.

There were many NoWait success stories. Carrie would have loved to caution these folks to be careful. Richard was no chemist, not that that had ever stopped him.

Oh, he had loved "inventing"—a love that had intensified after he'd gotten his degree, as if it gave him license to mix and match all kinds of herbs and chemicals.

The sad truth was, even his attempts to make salad dressing—"Look at Paul Newman, Carrie"—had been an unmitigated disaster. He had blown up the toilet in their first humble apartment trying to make a better, not to mention cheaper, cleaning solution.

At the time it had seemed funny and charming and rather exciting.

At the time just about everything had seemed funny and charming and rather exciting. Until the exact point their dreams had ended up on a collision course.

Already pregnant, Carrie had asked him one day when he would be ready to have children.

"Never," he'd said, and she had heard the truth in his voice, in the way he said that one word. He'd read the stunned expression on her face correctly, because he'd hastily added, "Well, maybe not *never* but certainly not now."

Sometimes, looking back, she wondered if she had pulled the plug too quickly. Certainly Dr. Terry Browell, that TV doctor who gave out such confident advice, probably would have thought so. Over the years she had wondered so often. Had she done the right thing? Had it really been her decision alone to make?

But in that moment, the word *never* shivering in the air between them, her husband had seemed like such a stranger to her, a man she had no hope of ever knowing, or ever holding.

She had gone on to marry a lovely man, Ralph Martin, now dead, not the least exciting, but never, ever a stranger to her.

And truth be told, Richard still seemed a stranger as she watched him today, performing, playing to his adoring public.

He stopped speaking suddenly and grinned.

Her heart stopped. Because suddenly he was not such a stranger. She had seen that very same grin for nearly twenty years.

In their son, Jason. And whenever Jason had grinned that grin, she had remembered the man who had given it to him.

Not the betrayals. Not the dreams on collision course.

The laughter. The lovemaking. The sheer joy of being together.

"Go after what you want," he repeated emphatically at the end of the seminar. "Erase self-doubt."

Carrie did not join the many who wanted to talk to him after the class. She slipped out the door and contemplated his words.

She smiled cynically. He would not have uttered

them nearly so confidently if he knew that what one member of his class wanted to go after was him. Oh, how she would love to expose Dr. Richard Strong for what he really was: a superficial man who had left his pregnant young wife to fend for herself. Who had emptied half the bank account when he had left.

Not, she thought reluctantly, that he had known she was pregnant.

That was the self-doubt part.

Erase it, she ordered herself. But she couldn't.

With Jason in college she had felt so confident that it was time to track down her old husband, to put away the ghosts of her old life for good.

She stood in the late-afternoon sunshine outside the Healthy Living Clinic. The door swung open, and a wave of laughing people, filled with confidence and energy and excitement from what they had just learned from Dr. Richie, spilled out on the sidewalk.

And her self-doubt intensified. She was no longer nearly as certain why she had come here or what she had hoped to accomplish. But a voice inside her, one of those ones that Dr. Richie spoke of but that she was pretty sure he was not on familiar terms with in his own life, told her to wait. When the time is right, you will know exactly what to do.

She walked away, feeling lonely and tense, and very, very separate from all the hopeful, energetic people who had been inspired by a man who was not even close to being what he was saying he was.

Five

For all the times she had looked longingly in the window, Maggie had never shopped in Classy Lass before.

The summer dress was still in the window, red and bold, and, taking a deep breath, Maggie went through the wide double oak and glass doors. It was quickly apparent that Classy Lass was not the kind of store she usually shopped in. It was more like walking into a very posh hotel lobby than a store. There were deep comfortable leather sofas, tasteful displays, wonderful little alcoves to explore.

A freckled, friendly girl introduced herself as Tracey and made Maggie feel warmly welcome. Tracey acted as though she had no idea Maggie did not belong in a shop that was not advertising the underwear special in aisle 9 over the PA system.

"Make yourself at home," she said, "and just ask me if you need anything."

After looking at the price tag on a leather bag hooked carelessly over the arm of one of the sofas, Maggie wanted to say what she needed was a dose of oxygen. For a moment she considered leaving, but then she took a deep breath and approached Tracey.

"I like the red dress in the window, but I don't see it on display anywhere else. Have you got it?" Maggie gave the woman her size, and crossed her fingers that they'd have it.

Tracey grinned without one little bit of condescension. "Only one perfect little red dress," she said. "You don't want to see everyone in Portland wearing a dress you paid eight hundred dollars for, do you?"

Maggie felt her jaw dropping. Eight hundred dollars? For a dress that looked as if it barely contained a yard of material? She had known Classy Lass was going to be expensive, but she had not expected it to be quite so far out of her price range.

The girl read her expression, and instead of looking haughty, she took on the look of a conspirator. "It doesn't hurt to try it on," she said, and before Maggie could protest, she was up in the window retrieving the dress. "It is your size."

A moment later, Maggie found herself in a huge fitting room with thick carpets and wall-to-wall mirrors. There was room for a leather armchair and a reading table heaped with fashion magazines. There was no sign on the door warning about the dangers of shoplifting, either.

It was madness for Maggie to be here, and yet even so, she found herself skinning out of her clothes eagerly. She had hated the outfit she was wearing ever since she had seen Luke eye it—and dismiss it—this morning. Camel had always been one of her favorite colors. Now, lying in a crumpled heap on the thick burgundy rug, her suit looked like leftover porridge.

She didn't even want to know what he might think of her plain cotton briefs and bra. Maggie slid the red dress over her head, and stood there for a minute with her eyes shut, not even wanting to look. The dress felt exquisite where it touched her skin, as light and feathery as a cloud.

Maggie opened her eyes and gasped.

The dress had been designed to show a woman at her very best. It looked deceptively simple, with its narrow spaghetti straps, snug bodice and a short skirt that swirled and lifted around her legs at the slightest movement.

She was not sure how but the dress managed to turn each of her faults into an asset. Her curviest areas, hips and chest, looked amazing, sensuous and full. When she twirled she saw how the flare of the skirt, the lightness of the fabric drew attention to the long, clean line of her leg.

It was the perfect summer dress, light, carefree, perky, flirty. It was a dress that celebrated all the mysteries and marvels and delights of being a woman.

But eight hundred dollars? She'd paid only slightly more than that for her wedding gown!

"Come show me," Tracey called.

Feeling as shy and as gauche as a farm girl fresh out of her overalls, Maggie emerged from the fitting room.

"Oh my God," the girl said, and Maggie knew it was no sales pitch.

"It's nice, isn't it?" she asked, twirling experimentally in front of another bank of floor-to-ceiling mirrors.

"Nice? Oh, no. It's not nice. It's naughty as hell, and if you don't buy it, you should have your head examined."

Maggie laughed. "I can't pay eight hundred dollars for a dress."

The girl eyed her shrewdly. "Let me guess. Working. Professional something, like a teacher or a nurse. Single."

"That all shows?" Maggie was going home and dumping the porridge suit in the garbage. She was unexciting and broadcasting it to the whole world!

"So, what do you spend your money on?" Tracey teased gently, "Your cat?"

"I don't have a cat," Maggie admitted.

"Well, then, you have absolutely no excuse not to treat yourself," Tracey said. "He won't be able to resist you."

"Who won't be able to resist me? A homeless cat looking to change his circumstances?" Maggie asked innocently.

"Nobody looks at a dress like that unless there's a *he* involved: human, male, ten-out-of-ten. Believe me. I've been working here a whole four months, and I know."

Maggie laughed. "I do believe you." She turned and looked in the mirror again. Well, why not buy the dress? Tracey was right. Maggie spent money on rent and had collected some lovely pieces of furniture. She treated herself to all her favorite romance authors' books, brand-new. She was saving for a down payment on a house. She had a car she adored.

But when did she ever spend money on just making herself feel good, beautiful, one hundred percent a woman? The Bold and Beautiful seminars didn't count!

And neither did the wedding that had not happened, but still had had to be paid for. Maggie realized that her non-wedding was the last time she had splurged on deliciously decadent things just for her. She had bought underwear and lingerie and sexy sundresses for the honeymoon on the Mexican Riviera that Darnel had gone on by himself. And had never returned from.

And when things had not worked out, she had packed up the items, unworn, most with the tags still on them, and sent them off to the Goodwill store.

What she hadn't realized until twenty-four hours ago, sprawled beneath a strange man's chest, was that she had packed up all that was feminine about herself, too. Her hopes and dreams, her longings and desires had suddenly seemed too fraught with danger to investigate any further. She had locked herself away from a world that held pain, like a princess in a tower. Or a social worker in an office.

"I'm going to take the dress," Maggie decided firmly. And not for Luke, either. For herself. She could sit out on her balcony at night, look at the waters of the Columbia River, just visible through a maze of other buildings, sip iced coffee and feel splendidly and sexily like a woman.

Okay, she planned to share that feeling of being womanly and sexy with Luke, but it was still for her.

It was time to begin the healing that she had never done.

"Want the bad news?" Tracey asked her.

"Eight hundred dollars isn't bad enough news?"

"I have some Jimmy Choos that are going to look divine with that."

"I'm scared to ask, but what the heck are Jimmy Choos?" Maggie asked.

A little while later she stood at the front desk with

the Jimmy Choo shoes, a shawl, new underwear and the dress all being packaged up for her.

"Now," the girl said when she was done folding everything carefully into tissue paper and putting it in boxes and then bags, "have you got the place picked out? To wear it?"

"I hadn't got that far," Maggie admitted. It occurred to her that if she played pool at Morgan's in this itty-bitty red dress the male heat in the place would probably set off the sprinkler system.

"I have an idea," Tracey said.

Maggie wondered if this funny freckle-faced girl was some sort of little angel sent to guide her through the pitfalls of trying to heal old wounds, find her inner woman, and just incidentally, get a man interested in her.

"It's just a suggestion, but have you heard of Heavenly Cup? The coffee and dessert bar?"

"I've walked by it a zillion times. I've never gone in."

"From the street you can't tell that they have this divine outdoor area with potted plants and trees, all lit up with white lights at night. It's right on the banks of the river. Tonight they're having a classical guitar concert on the patio. My boyfriend is playing, so I happen to be selling tickets. Inexpensive, so it balances out the dress. You can go and have coffee and dessert, and listen to the most beautiful music for under twenty bucks a person. And it does look like it's going to be a gorgeous night."

It did look like that. And Maggie had an absolute weakness for the classical guitar. But Luke at a classical guitar concert?

Well, why not?

She had moved into his arena last night, eating hamburgers and playing pool. Why not invite him to a place where she would feel comfortable?

A dessert bar! An evening of eating desserts was probably not the perfect date for a girl with way too much hip.

On the other hand, this dress did magical things to her hips, and there was always a little extra NoWait!

Maggie took a deep breath and dug back into her wallet. "Two tickets, please."

Tracey giggled. "I'm going to be there. I always try to watch Kenneth perform. But I can't wait to see you walk in with the guy you think is worth that dress."

Maggie laughed. This whole little interlude had seemed like the most pleasant and wonderful of adventures.

Is that what happened when you began to live your life more fully? When you went after what you wanted? When you tried to erase self-doubt?

She gathered her packages. "See you there," she said with breezy confidence that felt so good. But by the time she reached her car, her confidence was flagging.

Well, maybe she wouldn't see Tracey there, after all. She hadn't even asked Luke yet. It dawned on her he had the option of saying no. What if he had other plans?

Maggie, she told herself, the man is in the hospital. What other plans could he have?

He looked as if he might be one of those guys who was fanatical about sports. What if there was an important baseball game on TV? A baseball fan herself, she mentally reviewed the schedule, but couldn't remember a game of any importance. What if he just plain didn't want to go?

I am simply not accepting no for an answer, she thought, climbing into her car and stowing her packages behind the seat. That was part of the self-doubt, thinking she wasn't good enough for him, that somehow he was used to a different kind of woman and she didn't have a chance.

He had phoned her this morning, not the other way around. He was the one who had reopened a closed book. He was the one who had tangled their lives together just a little more deeply.

He still could have other plans, she told herself with a moan.

But as inexperienced as she was around men, Maggie knew one thing. All she had to do was show up at the hospital in that dress. If he had other plans, he'd change them.

It would take a bigger man than Luke August to resist her.

She giggled self-consciously. Good Lord. Maggie Sullivan playing the siren. The truth was she could hardly wait. And so she decided she would not phone and forewarn him; she would just show up in the dress and let it do its magic.

Hours later, she stepped out of her car in front of Portland General. Male heads turned as she sashayed up the walk. A nice man nearly tripped over himself trying to get to the door fast enough to open it for her.

The dress was summer itself—fun and sultry, playful and promising. It made her feel like a different person, outgoing and bold and carefree.

She discovered Luke in the TV room at the end of his hall, but he was unaware of her. Coming toward him, she could see he had on a plaid housecoat and slippers, and was leaning toward the TV, chin in hands, intently regarding the screen.

Her footsteps slowed as she regarded the picture he made. Aside from the fact that he looked like he could be doing the Christmas layout for GQ, it was a cozy picture of a man at home, relaxed, content with his life. Sunday morning. Newspapers scattered around, an old dog at his feet, a fire crackling in a hearth, the smell of bacon cooking.

But she already knew Luke August to be the man least likely to enjoy a relaxing moment in his housecoat and slippers.

Even so, the picture remained. In the background she almost heard the crackle of the bacon sizzling in the pan and the laughter of children at play.

Children? Oh God, she could not think of children and this man! Though Children's Connection had a fertility department, and Maggie knew there were many ways to make children these days, everyone tried the old-fashioned way first! If she let her mind wander too far down that road—making children the old-fashioned way with Luke August—she'd probably swoon again.

Despite her every effort not to think of Luke and children, in her mind's eye, green-eyed little boys with dark hair and freckles and grins full of mischief and liveliness materialized.

Maggie felt like a fraud. How could she go to Luke in a dress like this, when she harbored a dream like that in the back of her mind? A dream she hadn't even acknowledged she had, a dream of domestic bliss and contentment that Luke August, certified daredevil, would never fit into?

Trying to banish the green-eyed children, and with her heart in her throat, Maggie turned to walk away before he caught sight of her.

"Hey."

Too late. The red dress had worked against her and must have caught his attention. She turned slowly back to him.

He looked at her, shook his head and then looked again. He got to his feet and stared at her. If they were sharing that cozy little scene of her imagination, from the smoldering look in his green eyes, there would be some burned bacon and children sent out to the yard to play.

"Maggie," he croaked.

She had to get a hold of herself. She could not allow the boundaries of fantasy and reality to melt together.

She was a vision of feminine allure, and she knew it, the dress skimming around her, her hair falling in a rich cascade over a shawl that played peekaboo with the creaminess of her naked shoulders.

She watched it all register in his eyes. She took a deep breath. Run or take the plunge? Her whole problem was she took everything way too seriously.

A date did not a marriage and children make! She was not a starry-eyed sixteen-year-old, and the Cinderella notions of a handsome prince, glass slippers and happily ever after had to go!

Though, forcing her mind to take lighter roads, she doubted the glass slipper had anything on Jimmy Choo, including price.

"I wondered if you'd like to go out with me tonight, Luke," she said.

He folded his arms over the deepness of his chest and

rocked back on his heels. A man just had no right to look that sexy in a robe and slippers.

"We weren't going to see each other," he reminded her. "You said. I thought—"

She moved toward him, put her finger on his lips and looked up at him through lashes darkened with mascara. "Don't think," she said huskily.

She thought he might start laughing at her imitation of a woman so confident in her own skin, but he didn't. He gulped.

"I'll go get ready."

She smiled.

"And meet you at the back door?" he asked.

She shook her head and brandished a white piece of paper. "I got you a pass."

"You can do that? Get passes?"

"If you know the right people."

"And wear a dress like that," he muttered. "Give me ten minutes."

He gave her one more quick, loaded look, and then staggered off like a man who had stood much too close to an exploding bomb.

Luke went into his room, shut the door and leaned on it. He closed his eyes and took a deep, steadying breath. When he opened his eyes again, he found himself looking straight at Nurse Nightmare. He let out a little yelp.

"I understand you have a pass," she said to him with deep disapproval, apparently having forgotten how prepared she was to cozy up to him this morning when she had wanted something on Billy's behalf.

"Yeah. I understand that, too."

"Maggie Sullivan is one of the sweetest girls you could ever meet," Nurse Nightmare informed him through pursed lips.

He should just open the door and give the nurse a little look at how her sweet little Maggie had turned to spicy in the blink of an eye. Five-alarm spicy, in fact. But he didn't. He just said, "Yes, ma'am. I understand that."

"Do you?" Her tone was etched with disbelief. She was giving him the insensitive lunkhead look.

He didn't say anything. He wanted her to get out of here so he could throw on some clothes and have another look at Maggie. He moved by her and looked through the wardrobe-style closet at the side of his bed.

"She's been hurt before."

He'd already guessed, and didn't want to know. But reluctantly, he turned and gave the nurse his full attention.

"There's an expression about being left standing at the altar, though very few people have had to experience that literally. But she did. Arrived at the church in her gorgeous gown and the whole entourage, and all the guests seated, only to find no groom."

Luke had to turn swiftly back to the wardrobe to hide the expression on his face. He was sure it would scare the nurse, because he felt murderous. He could not believe the white-hot surge of rage that he felt. He could not believe someone could do that to Maggie. Or to anyone.

But mostly to Maggie. He had seen the goodness of her, the purity of her soul, when she had talked to Billy today. What kind of ass could do that to someone like her?

Okay, Luke was no fan of the institution of marriage,

but at least he was up front about that from the second things started looking serious.

And here Maggie was, in her red dress, trying to put her life back together again. Her bravery was touching and heart-wrenching and scary as hell.

Why pick on Luke August? Couldn't she see he was the least likely guy to be able to help her ever trust the male half of the human race again? Apparently Nurse Nightmare could see that simple truth!

"Does she have a penchant for insensitive lunkheads or what?" he asked, trying to keep his tone light. He failed. There was a snarl of barely leashed anger in it.

"That's the thing. Darnel worked at Children's Connection. Many of us knew them both, at least professionally. He seemed to be a very nice man."

Unspoken in the air between them hung the remainder of her thought. *Not like you.*

Luke thought Darnel was going to be a very nice man with a rearranged face if he ever had the happy opportunity to meet him in a dark alley. No, scratch the dark alley. He'd settle for the opportunity.

"When did it happen?" he asked, trying to keep his tone casual, his teeth clenched together so hard his jaw hurt.

"Two years ago. No, three. The whole hospital talked of nothing else for months."

He felt angry again at the thought of Maggie trying to hold her head up high with everyone talking about her.

But three years ago? That wasn't nearly as bad as if it had happened last week. Surely she was over the worst of it now. It wasn't as if he was being entrusted with a newly bruised heart, a soul freshly ravaged.

He heard the door open and shut behind him, and

knew the nurse, her warning delivered, had left him to mull it over. He picked a pair of dark cords and a sports shirt out of his limited choices and went into the bathroom for a quick shower and a shave.

A woman in a red dress.

Really, a red dress gave about the simplest message in the whole world to a man. There was something primal about it, sexy and seductive.

But on Maggie Sullivan? Absolutely nothing was simple about her. He should just hang a white flag out the door. He should tell her he wasn't going anywhere with her.

But, just like last night, he had this almost irresistible desire to make her laugh, to make her forget some of the secrets and sorrows that made her eyes so somber.

"Wrong man for the job," he said slapping his freshly shaved face with cologne.

But it occurred to him that was twice today his nemesis, Nurse Nightmare, had trusted him with very delicate assignments.

What had she said this morning? Oh, yeah. Require more of yourself.

And so tonight, that was what he would do. Luke August, who had a gift for impersonation, would impersonate the perfect gentleman. He would escort Maggie wherever she wanted to go, and he would make sure she had fun. He would not mess with her broken heart. That meant no on-fire kiss goodnight.

A better man would not have felt such sharp regret.

Outside the hospital, Maggie handed him the keys to her car.

"Are you sure?" he asked. "I've been known to wreck

all manner of things with engines. Even my lawn mower can't keep up with me."

"I'm sure," she said.

He sighed inwardly. Okay, she was bent on trusting him, and he was determined to be a gentleman about it. He held open her door for her, but seeing that red dress ride up her knee when she sat down weakened his resolve.

And when he got in the other side of her tiny car and smelled that scent that was all hers—citrus with an underlying shade of musk—his resolve weakened some more. He knew a great place to go on a night like this. A rocky beach where they could be alone.

"Turn left here," she directed him.

He could keep going straight, but her voice did not match the dress or her fragrance. Her voice was nervous, like a schoolgirl going to the prom. He wondered what she had in store for him, and reminded himself he was on his best behavior.

Not that his best behavior had ever been that good.

She directed him to a place called the Heavenly Cup. It was a coffee bar in a remodeled sandstone. Once they were inside, they were directed across the room to where wall-to-wall French doors opened onto a yard at the back, full of potted trees and little white lights and wrought-iron tables. They were close to the bank of the river, and he could see its dark waters moving, reflecting the lights of downtown Portland.

"Not my regular kind of place," he teased her. "Where's the sawdust on the floor? Is the pool table hidden somewhere? Can I get a beer?"

"You don't drink beer," she reminded him. "Actually, I've never been here before, either."

Despite that, it was her kind of place, he could tell. The crisp linen tablecloths, the nice lights in the trees, the fresh flowers on the tables, the murmur of the river in the background. The place had an ambience of romance.

"There's a concert here tonight," she said. "I thought you might like it."

A freckle-faced girl came over to their table and whispered something in Maggie's ear that made her blush.

"This is Tracey, Luke."

He took Tracey's hand, and the girl turned and smiled at Maggie. "Off the scale," she said. "Do you think it was worth it?"

"Worth what?" he asked Maggie.

"Oh," the girl said before Maggie could answer, "here's Kenneth now."

A guy came out of the restaurant and sauntered up to them. He had long blond hair in dreadlocks and jeans with a hole in the knee, and the look he gave the freckle-faced girl, and the one she returned to him, reminded Luke, almost painfully, what it was like to be young and brand-new to the world of passion.

He glanced at Maggie. She had seen that look, too, and longing passed, brief and bright, through her eyes before she looked quickly away.

"Kenneth is the musician tonight," Tracey said proudly. Then she looped her arm through his and escorted him to a small raised podium set back amongst the light-spangled trees.

Given Kenneth's appearance, Luke hoped for some good ol' rock 'n' roll, but that was probably dating himself. The kid probably rapped or did head-banging or something similar.

Though Luke couldn't imagine Maggie would go for either style of music.

With his girlfriend beaming her love from the front table, the kid picked up the guitar that was leaning casually against the stool on the stage. He leaned his fanny on the stool and bent his head over the instrument. Then his fingers began to do a dance over the strings.

"This is for Tracey," Kenneth said as he cast her a heated look. "It's called 'Love on a Summer Night.'"

In a moment the small space shimmered with the beauty of that music.

Maggie's hand crept across the table and Luke took it. No worries about butter tonight, apparently.

He'd expected to be bored. Instead, the most amazing thing happened. His mind—or maybe it was more his soul—opened to the music. He was stunned by the gentle and glowing beauty of it. Who would have thought Luke August could be so taken with a sound? Or that his world had somehow become so narrow that this sound was new to him?

He would have thought no one would ever accuse him of being the kind of man who did not explore his horizons.

He pushed boundaries all the time. Boundaries of speed and strength, muscle and sheer determination pitted against the laws of physics. But that was his world, and somehow he had stopped venturing into worlds beyond it.

He glanced at Maggie. Her expression was rapt, her eyes glowing softly as she let the music wash over her.

He had a feeling that if he let this thing with Maggie go anywhere she would take him to places he had never been before.

Places of the soul.

Places of the heart.

Places of deep longing that would expose the loneliness at his core.

It seemed the guitar was finding that place, the melody haunting, exquisitely tender, making Luke *feel* exactly what the title of the song had promised.

Love on a summer night. The boy's fingers plucked and danced and stroked, and coaxed from his guitar not music but love, shimmering with hope and pathos and pain and glory.

Luke had never had any desire to go to such places. Amber would not have brought him to a place like this. No, jukeboxes loaded with old Springsteen tunes would be more her style. Peanut shells on the floor, dancing on the tables as the night grew wilder.

Despite the promise of Maggie's red dress, Luke had a feeling this was as wild as things were getting tonight.

Thank God. He could not stand the contradictions posed by Maggie. The complications. How could she wear a dress like that, and then bring him to a place of his soul instead of his libido?

She obviously had no idea that this was a game men and women played, and that it had rules. He was willing to forgo his vow to show her a fun time. It was replaced with a desire just to get out of here alive.

The dessert tray came. He ordered one of everything on it. Speed wasn't the only way to stuff back uncomfortable feelings of confusion and yearning mixed. Besides, it was the kind of gesture that would have dismayed his well-bred mother.

Maggie seemed to think it was hilarious, and she

laughed. Just as it had done last night, her laughter transformed her and chased some of the seriousness from her. So, he was going to get her laughing after all.

An hour later it occurred to him that eating too many sweets was a dumb plan for trying to get out of this evening intact. He had just eaten a dessert called death by chocolate and he was pretty sure that was going to be his fate.

But better that than death by innocent girl in a red dress. He glanced up at her. She had a little ring of chocolate around her own mouth and looked adorable in her distress when she looked down at all the empty dessert plates.

She excused herself rapidly.

Watching her hurry off, he hoped she wasn't one of those types who had to puke after they ate. No, she had too many delicious round curves to have that particular disorder. All he noticed when she came back was that the subtle fragrance of citrus and musk that seemed to be all hers was stronger.

"Are you ready to go?" she asked.

"No. I just have to have another death by chocolate."

She laughed and started to reach for her wallet.

He put his hand over hers. "Excuse me?"

"I invited you," she said. "It'll be my treat."

"Over my dead body. Which, you might have noticed the death by chocolate hasn't quite accomplished yet."

"You paid last night at Morgan's."

"Maggie, I'm an old-fashioned kind of guy."

He didn't know what it was about the word *old-fashioned* that made her cheeks glow that sexy shade of red that nearly matched her dress, but he liked it.

He liked so much about her. He liked the softness of her face under the glow of these outdoor lights. He liked the color of her eyes. He liked her laughter. He liked the richness of her hair. He liked her depth and her sensitivity.

And he liked that dress.

"Yeah, I'm ready to go," he said gruffly.

He drove again, aware of her expectation that he might drive somewhere quiet, like that beach he had thought of earlier.

But Luke was well aware something very dangerous was going on inside him. This was the kind of woman—complex, deep, smart, beautiful—that a man could get into real trouble with.

She was the type of woman a man could fall in love with.

Not him, of course, he didn't do the love thing. And he didn't do it because he had the good sense to see it coming.

He pulled into the hospital parking lot.

"Thanks, Maggie. That was—"

Before he could even brace himself she had thrown herself in his lap. Her arms were wrapped around his neck and her lips were laying claim to his.

His vow to be a gentleman was just that! Words, a desire. The vow could not withstand this kind of test.

How could he be a gentleman, when she intended to be a hellcat?

He took what she was offering. He took the softness of her lips and the velvet of her tongue. He allowed himself to delight in the soft swell of her breast squeezed up hard against his chest, the roundness of her buttocks and the softness of her upper thigh where they rested on him.

He had envied, briefly, that young musician and his girlfriend tonight, envied the newness of the world of men and women that they were exploring.

And yet he was aware that this encounter had a new flavor to it, too. There was a dimension here that he had not experienced often.

What was it? Tenderness?

Innocence.

The word exploded in his brain, and he put Maggie off his lap and glared at her. Her hair was a wild tangle. Her breasts heaved with desire under the line of that red dress. Her lips were puffy and her eyes were glazed with desire.

He looked away, ran a hand through his hair.

Luke realized he could not allow himself to be fooled by the boldness of her kisses. She was Maggie Mouse, sweet and shy, and much too vulnerable a girl for a rough guy like him.

"You were right the first time," he said, and was amazed it was taking all his strength to say it. "We can't see each other again, Maggie."

Her name felt like that music coming off his lips, haunting and beautiful. He dared look at her, but looked swiftly away.

He had to make her get this: it wasn't going to work. She was too soft and too sensitive. No matter what that dress said, she was a picket-fence kind of girl. The kind of girl you said forever to, or nothing at all.

"I'm going home tomorrow," he said. "I'm being discharged."

He hazarded another look at her. She wasn't getting it. Her eyes were still wide and filled with light.

It occurred to him they were half in love with each other already. That was the light he saw in her eyes, tender and smoldering.

It made him panic. He had to push her away somehow so that she was never coming back, never hoping, never dreaming.

"I'm going home to my roommate. Her name is Amber."

The silence was choked. He glanced at her. She was looking stiffly straight ahead, but her hands were knitting and unknitting on her lap.

"You live with someone?" she asked, and her voice was small and broken, and he knew he had accomplished exactly what he wanted.

"She hangs around," he said.

"Could you get out of my car now?"

He didn't say anything else. He got out of the car. He felt like the worst kind of creep. She thought he'd gone out with her when he was committed to someone else.

It was a lie and a monstrous one, but he'd told it for her own good.

She didn't even get out of the car, just scooted across from the passenger seat to the driver's.

She ducked her head so that her hair fanned out over her cheeks, but he had seen the truth. She was crying.

He had made Miss Maggie Mouse cry.

It should have felt like a confirmation. As if he had done exactly the right thing. Maggie was way too soft for him. He would hurt her without meaning to.

A sharp, quick cut was better than a slow, lingering tear.

But if he'd done the right thing, why did he feel like

such a jerk? As if life had given him one good thing and he had tossed it away.

He watched the Beetle until he could see it no longer, and then he shoved his hands in his pockets and went up the stairs of the hospital. He felt a hundred years old, and he didn't think it had a thing to do with the physio workout he'd done today.

Six

"**Y**ou're fired. Get the hell off my job," Luke said. He watched, his arms folded over his chest, his legs planted solidly, as his former employee shot him one dark, challenging look, reconsidered and then scurried away.

Luke turned to where he had caught the man smoking behind a pallet of plywood, and disgustedly stomped out the still-smoldering butt.

"Ah, boss?"

"Yeah?" Luke turned and glared at Brian, aware that firing the man who had been irritating him for three whole hours now had not taken the edge off his black mood. Not even a little bit.

Brian was his best employee and a pretty good buddy, too. They'd been working together more than six years, which was a long time in this industry.

"That's the third guy you've fired in the three days since you've been back at work."

"It was not his coffee break. Besides, he screwed the dog—" he said, using the vulgar construction-site term for lazy. *There, Maggie, that's what kind of man I really am.* He could just picture her, her little Maggie Mouse ears turning to crimson at words like that.

Amber would use words like that, he thought.

"Who's Amber?" Brian asked baffled.

Had he said that out loud? "I didn't say Amber...." He improvised. "I said *anger.* As in that guy I just canned really pissed me off. He's been pissing me off since he got here. How long did he work for me?"

"Since this morning."

"He was a lousy worker. I think he was scared of heights, too. Did you see him tiptoeing along that outside wall?"

Brian did not look convinced. "Is everything okay?" he finally ventured cautiously.

"Oh, jim-dandy. I've got to get this place locked up by the end of next week, and I can't find a crew that's worth a damn."

"I didn't mean about the job," he said. "You don't seem right since you got out of the hospital. Are you in pain or something?"

Oh, yeah, he was in pain. But it wasn't physical. Or not all physical. It was the pain of a man who was carrying around a phantom woman inside him, a woman who watched him with huge, soft eyes, and cringed from his language, and laughed at his jokes and cried at the slightest provocation.

Though telling her he lived with another woman was not exactly a *slight* provocation, even in his book.

"No," he snapped when he became aware Brian was studying him with a concerned look. Concerned looks were not welcome on the construction site. "I'm not in pain. Now get to work, or you'll be following that guy down the road."

"You watch how you talk to me, or *I will* be following him down the road. Gladly."

They stood glaring at each other for a minute.

"Sorry," Luke finally said. Sighing, he pushed his fingers through his hair. He'd always been difficult to work for. He expected the same of his crew that he asked of himself. He was a perfectionist and he drove himself hard. He didn't want to lose Brian because he was in a temper over Maggie.

Brian stood his ground for a minute longer, then shook it off. "You know, boss, if I didn't know you better, I'd say it was a girl."

"If I didn't know you better, I'd say it was a girl," Luke repeated, imitating Brian's voice with annoyance as he walked into his house an hour later, tossed his tool belt off in the back entry hall, and slammed his lunch pail down. "Sure. A girl."

He went up the few steps from the back entry to the kitchen. The house was just outside the metropolis of Portland, in Clackamas County, in a satellite community called Boring. Even Luke was aware of the irony. His house was a 1970s split-level on an acre of land with a great shop out back. He bought these places, fixer-uppers, renovated them and turned them over. He'd extensively remodeled the kitchen on this particular house, and usually he enjoyed coming in the back door to the new raised panel white cabinets, hardwood floor, kitchen island, the big new window that looked out to Mount Hood.

Tonight the kitchen seemed oppressive.

"The heat. Maybe central air next," he thought, though the average heat in July in this part of Oregon hovered around seventy-nine degrees, which hardly warranted air conditioning.

Planning projects was easier than thinking about what he had done to his life four days ago when he had told Maggie he was going home to his roommate.

Luke was acutely aware tonight of what was wrong with the kitchen. There were no smells of food cooking, no flowers on the table, no magnets on the fridge.

There were none of those little touches that signaled a woman in residence, little touches that could clear oppression out of the air like smoke before a fan.

The truth was there had never been a woman in residence here. There hadn't even been any overnighters. It was his space, and he protected it. Nobody told him to pick up his clothes or tried to sew curtains for that new window.

He flipped on the light of the newly installed sunshine ceiling, and realized there was a woman in residence, after all. Amber beamed at him from her place of honor on the wall by the phone. He grabbed a soda out of the fridge, popped the lid and sidled over to study her.

"You aren't the cooking, flowers, magnets-on-the-fridge, sew-drapes, pick-up-your-clothes kind of girl anyway, are you, honey?"

He'd never wanted that. Ever. Wild in the bedroom

would do for his ideal woman. The sad truth was, he'd had plenty of that.

And it had always proved less than ideal. So much so that he'd retreated from the whole world of even superficial relationships for a long, long time. Which explained why no one had ever been here. Or no one of the opposite sex. Of course, his buddies dropped by all the time. They spent time out in the huge shop working on motorcycles, and they all enjoyed the freedom of coming in for a beer after. No one to nag about grease in the sink, or booted feet propped up on the coffee table. Oh, yeah, the buddies loved it here.

And then they all went home to magnets on the fridge.

Well, maybe someday he would, too.

"When I find you, Amber," he promised. He kissed his fingers and planted them in the curve of her décolletage. Normally that would have given him a bit of a chuckle. Tonight it struck him as a sadly pathetic thing to do.

Come to think of it, Luke had always liked this kitchen just fine, too. Brian had been uncomfortably close to the truth. Something *was* wrong, and it *was* about a female.

Not a damn girl, either. A woman. Luke had given up a real woman—one who looked absolutely fabulous in a curve-hugging red dress—for this? Kissing a calendar and the privilege of washing greasy hands in the kitchen sink without being yelled at?

But from the way Maggie had kissed, would she be both? A cooking, flowers, magnets-on-the-fridge kind of girl and breath-stoppingly sexy, too? Or was she just playing at being wildly sexy? What if she was everything? Smart and sexy? Beautiful and decent?

"Well, what if she is?" he muttered. "With a girl like her those kisses could end up costing, big time." There was always the price, and the price would be she'd want to tame him, for one. They all wanted to tame him.

"Oh, Lukie," he mimicked a female voice and batted his eyelashes, "you aren't going to go ride your motorcycle instead of picking out wallpaper, are you?" Blink-blink.

And after she sewed curtains she probably wouldn't want to sell the place, no matter what the profits would be. No, siree, she'd want to *nest*. She'd want a picket fence to replace the overgrown hedge that surrounded his place, and eventually she'd be eyeing up a little swing set that would have to be moved every time he mowed the lawn. And thinking about the lawn, she'd probably want that mowed quite a bit more frequently than it was now.

A swing set? Now he was thinking of kids and Maggie! Total confirmation that he had cut his losses at exactly the right time.

"Stop thinking about Maggie," he ordered himself. It was an order he'd already disobeyed at least half a dozen times today.

The phone rang, and he picked it up before the first ring had completed, aware that his heart was beating wildly, that he *wanted* it to be her, the one he wasn't thinking about.

"Hello?"

"Luke, darling, it's Mother."

He wished he'd invested in caller ID. "Hi, Mom."

"You didn't tell me you were out of the hospital. I went to visit you today."

"The announcement card is in the mail," he said. He winked at Amber.

"Oh, Luke."

How did he manage to elicit that tone no matter what he did? If he'd told her he was leaving the hospital, he would have got the same thing for leaving too soon.

It was always unspoken between them. *Oh, Luke. You can disrupt my life without half trying.*

See, Maggie? he said inwardly. I saved you from myself. A disruptive, unreliable, risk-taking guy who doesn't have any patience with his own mother. Luke knew Maggie wouldn't like that.

But Amber wouldn't care.

"How is Amber?" his mother asked.

"Fine," he said, careful as always not to say enough that his mother caught on that Amber was largely fictional.

"I'd love to meet her sometime."

"Hmm," he said, noncommittally.

"And could you and I get together for lunch soon?"

"Why?"

"I haven't seen you for a while."

He closed his eyes. His mother had not seen him for most of his childhood—unless she was driving him to the hospital after another one of his accidents. Even that chore seemed to fill her with resentment, her child getting in the way of *her* life of hair appointments and charity balls and afternoon "tea" at the club. Tea that somehow made her breath smell like alcohol.

Last year she'd gotten into a twelve-step group and therapy and God knows what else. Now she was always trying to fix things between them.

He was thirty-four years old. He didn't need a mommy anymore, thanks. Still, he found it hard to say no to Annabelle August. She was trying so hard. It was annoying as hell, but she was trying.

"You saw me in the hospital a couple of times," he reminded her.

"That's not private," she said.

He refrained, barely, from groaning. Luke hated it when she wanted *private* meetings between them. It meant she was going to try and probe his childhood wounds some more, drag herself over the coals for all the things not said and not done. She was making her way, painfully, through the years. She hadn't even gotten to Stinkbomb, yet.

Maggie would probably approve of his going out for lunch with his mother.

I don't give a flying chicken what Maggie cares about, he thought stubbornly, but he knew his last-minute substitution of the word *chicken* for his more favored choice, even in the privacy of his own mind, meant that he did.

"Prelude's at noon? Tuesday?" His mother's voice was all sugar and hope.

"Mom," he said patiently, "I work. And not in a suit. You don't want me showing up at Prelude's at noon on Tuesday, believe me. We're pouring concrete. It is not pretty. The maître d' will frown at mud on the carpets, holes in my jeans and my hands."

"Your hands?"

"Concrete eats holes in your hands if you touch it wet."

"Then why do you?"

Another happy phrase from his childhood. Only then it had been, Why do you do this to *me?*

Why did he do anything? Why did he drive too fast and leap motorcycles over ravines? Because he was impulsive, that's why. And impatient. Driven. Because there was a hole in him, and not in his hands, big enough to drive a cement truck through, that he kept trying to fill.

"You're back at work?" his mother said when he didn't answer her other questions.

"Uh, yeah."

"But that can't be good for your back. Darling, it's way too soon. Let me slip a little money into your account."

Let me look after you. Let me be there.

Was there a nice way to tell her it was too late? No, there wasn't. Besides, he wasn't back at work because he needed money. He was back at work because he needed to be busy, to keep his mind off *things*. According to Brian he wasn't really succeeding.

"I don't need money," he said, trying for a patient note. "I make good money." She seemed to have it set in her head that because he got dirty at work and had to use muscle he was just squeaking by in the financial department. Though in terms of his family dynasty, his earning power would be considered small potatoes, but Luke was satisfied.

Aside from the residential construction business that he owned and operated, he had an eye for houses that needed a bit of work. He fixed them up in his spare time and turned them over for a profit.

The money kept stacking up in his bank account, much more than a man of his simple needs required. His biggest expense was motorcycle parts. And medical insurance.

Of course, if there was a picket fence and a swing set in his future, that could change in a heck of a hurry.

There is no picket fence or swing set in your future, he told himself roughly.

"There's no what in your future, dear?"

"No lunch at Prelude's," he said firmly.

"Oh," she said, her voice small and hurt.

"Look, there's a little pub close to where I'm working. I think it's called Marcy's. I could meet you on Wednesday for a quick lunch."

"Oh," she said again, happily this time, as if he'd given her a million-dollar diamond bracelet to match her million-dollar diamond earrings. "I'll be there."

He sighed and looked at the phone. She'd hung up before he had a chance to tell her to leave the diamonds, stiletto heels and Chanel suit at home. But then who was he to tell his mother how to dress? Or anything else, for that matter.

"Something else to look forward to," he told Amber glumly as he marked the date on the calendar next to her, which was current. He polished off his soda and crushed the can in his hand.

Amber liked juvenile displays of masculine strength. He studied Amber's picture. She was as perfect as ever, wasn't she?

But tonight he noticed the black of her eyes was not a true black. Maybe dark brown. In fact, on close inspection, her eyes looked vapid and a little bit vacant. If she ever cried because someone told her a lie about being committed to someone else, she'd look like a mime with her two tons of black mascara running down her face.

But what was he thinking? Amber wouldn't cry over something like that. She'd probably clunk him over the head with a beer bottle, which was about what he deserved.

He continued to study her in a strange new light.

Amber's bottom lip looked a little too puffy; she either bit it repeatedly or had had collagen injected into it. And she was pretty skinny in other places, so it was probably a whole pile of silicone spilling out of that black leather jacket. Her hair was a shade of brassy copper that could only come out of a bottle and her lipstick was way too red.

He had never looked at Amber with such a critical spirit before. It was with great disappointment that he admitted Amber looked as phony as a three-dollar bill. She probably didn't even know how to ride that gorgeous bike—exactly the same model as his—that she was leaning over!

He grabbed the calendar off the wall and slammed it facedown onto his kitchen table. He had a zillion real girls he could call if he wanted company.

He had a drawer by the phone full of little scraps of paper and business cards and bar napkins with numbers scrawled on them. He went over and pulled open the drawer, pawed through it, trying to attach faces to names. Tiffany. Brittany. Sandy. Gail. Paula. Joan.

He slammed the drawer back shut.

Every single one of them suddenly struck him as being as phony as Amber. He wasn't sure he could tell them apart. Grabbing another soda, he headed out the back door.

"Sorry, honey," he called. "Our first fight."

Once upon a time it was a great source of amusement to him to talk to Amber. Now it just seemed silly. Pathetic.

He went across his backyard, which indeed needed mowing since he had been in hospital for a couple of weeks, to his detached shop, a big barn of a building perfect for working on all sorts of motorized machines, and for storing all those collectibles that went with motorized machines, like nuts and bolts and spare seats, extra windshields, chrome pipes and parts.

He unlocked the shop door and turned on the light. He took a deep breath of the air in there. It smelled good, that wonderful old garage smell, kind of dank and musty, with overlays of oil and metal and all things manly.

His street bike had been hauled here by somebody after the accident, and since he had arrived home, Luke had been finding refuge in here, unbending metal, making lists of parts, sorting through buckets of oily bolts. In a moment, forgetting he had not had anything to eat, he was up to his elbows in thick black grease.

He even started whistling, but after a while he realized it wasn't "What Do You Do With a Drunken Sailor?"

At first, he was not even sure what it was. He stopped pulling the wrench, whistled a few bars experimentally and found them sad and haunting and ultimately hopeful.

"Love on a Summer Night."

He groaned and, heedless of the grease on his fingers, he went over and turned on his radio, fiddled with the tuning dial until he found a real head-banger special.

If he listened carefully he could discern the words.

In effect the singer, if that merciless shouting could be called singing, thought life was not nice, would not get better, that it sucked every single day and then you died. This message was interspersed with enough curse words to make even a hardened construction worker like himself feel faintly uncomfortable.

Maggie wouldn't like—

He stopped himself. The song, after all, summed up the state of his own life rather nicely. But when he tried to hum along, he couldn't get the tune.

"Maggie," Kristen said, "what on earth is wrong with you? That's the third time in less than an hour that I've asked you a question and gotten a blank look. Are you ill?"

"No."

"I didn't think so. You're not eating as if you're ill."

Maggie had tried to avoid Kristen for this very reason. Her best friend always saw way too much. But Kristen had a nose for something being wrong, and today she hadn't taken no for an answer about a lunch date.

At least Maggie had talked her out of Morgan's Pub!

"Thanks for noticing I'm eating well," Maggie said glumly. If she kept it up, shortly she would no longer fit into that red dress.

And that was a good thing, wasn't it? That dress only reminded her of the woman she had thought she could pretend to be. And had failed so miserably to be.

She had even stopped using the NoWait. What did she care if she turned into a one-ton hippo?

This morning she had retrieved her camel-colored suit from the bag destined for Goodwill. She'd let it hang beside the shower, and the worst of the wrinkles had come out of it. She had put it on, resigned to who she really was.

"Maggie! The question? What is wrong with you? If you aren't ill, what's the matter?"

"I'm fine," Maggie said. "Sorry, I'm just distracted."

"Distracted? You look like hell. You're eating like a horse. You're body is in this room with me, but your mind is not. Gosh, if I didn't know you better, I'd say it was a man."

Maggie was silent.

"Oh, God," Kristen said, "it's a man."

Maggie sighed and took a deep drink of her non-diet soda.

"What is going on? How can you have a man in your life without me knowing about it?"

"His name's Luke," Maggie said, "Luke August." The words started to flow out of her like rainwater out of a barrel that had been shot full of holes.

It felt disgustingly good to be purging herself. In her own ears it sounded ridiculous—that she'd asked a man out on the strength of him running her over in a wheelchair. She sounded like a teenager, hopelessly infatuated with a man she knew nothing about.

Of course, the extent to which she had known nothing about him had only become shockingly clear to her a few nights ago. She was still dazed by it, by how wrong she had been about him.

"He had a girlfriend," she finished her sad tale, licking the last remnants of chocolate drizzle from her cheesecake off her fork. "Live-in. He went out with me, and then, when he was released from the hospital, he went home to her."

"No," Kristen said, incensed. "The snake!"

"That's right," Maggie said with a sad shake of her head. "The snake."

Kristen regarded her through narrowed eyes, and then declared, "You still have feelings for him!" The tone was definitely accusatory.

"Believe me, I'm trying not to." It was true. Maggie

was doing her best to feel righteously angry, betrayed, scorned. Instead she would think of his eyes caressing her, and his lips, and feel a chasm of loneliness open up inside her.

"Trying is not good enough," Kristen said. "Tell me he is banished, Maggie. Banished."

"Kristen, I just can't believe I could have read him so wrong."

"That is not banished!" Kristen looked at her sadly. "Honey, you seem to have a talent for reading men wrong."

Wasn't that just the understatement of the century? "This was different, Kristen, I felt as if I knew him. As if I had always known him. I trusted him so completely."

"Didn't you feel that way about Darnel?"

"Kristen, I have never felt this way." It was true. She had felt safe with Darnel, comfortable. He'd been like a favorite rocking chair, or a warm bath on a chilly evening. Unexciting, but comforting, soothing.

"Tell me how you feel," Kristen said.

"When I was with him I felt as if I had awakened from a long sleep. Life seemed to sizzle with possibilities it had never had before. Kristen, I felt as if I was on fire with life, ready to throw wide my arms and embrace the whole world."

It sounded ridiculously poetic when said out loud, and Kristen looked suitably cynical. "You cannot be in love with a snake!" she said, horrified. "There are lots of men out there, for God's sake. How about Donald Anderson?"

"Do I know a Donald Anderson?"

"He's an ordinary-looking guy who takes the Bold and Beautiful seminar with us. He looks so nice."

Maggie was pretty sure she'd seen Donald playing

tonsil hockey with someone in Morgan's. Besides, how did you settle for ordinary after you'd had extraordinary? Being with someone like Luke set a whole new standard.

"Maggie, you have to be careful of those handsome men. They are just too used to getting their own way. Having women throw themselves at them."

"It's a moot point now. No more handsome men for me. And no more Bold and Beautiful seminars," she announced. "And I'm not using the NoWait. I'm accepting my lot in life. I'm not trying for the new improved Maggie anymore."

"Oh, Maggie."

"Don't feel sorry for me. After Darnel, I've had all the pity I can handle for one lifetime. I want to go live a quiet life in a convent now."

"A convent? With nuns? Maggie!"

"Don't worry. They appear to prefer Catholics."

"You checked?"

"You can find anything on the Internet, even convents. Unfortunately they are retreat centers, not recruiting projects for the brokenhearted. I can't even run off and join the convent. My sense of failure is complete."

"Nonsense," Kristen said. "We're going to see Dr. Richie right this second. His advice got you into the predicament and he can advise you how to get out of it."

"I'd rather have another piece of cheesecake."

"No."

Her broken heart seemed to have made her very pliable, because before she knew exactly what had happened, Kristen had locked her elbow in a firm grip and was marching her down the street and toward the Healthy Living Clinic.

Suddenly, confessing all to Dr. Richie, with his

warm, sympathetic eyes, seemed to be the most inviting of scenarios.

She had a feeling that Luke wouldn't approve, but
then who cared what he approved of or didn't? He was
a snake. And no longer part of her life.

"Dr. Richie, Maggie Sullivan is here. She wondered
if you had a moment."

Richard tried not to flinch at being called Dr. Richie
by his receptionist. Almost everyone called him that
now! He had thought he was going to get used to it, but
he hadn't…yet. Really he should never have allowed it
to start. The nickname was disrespectful of his true title
and accomplishments.

Of course Dr. Terry Browell let people address him
by his title and first name. Richard blamed his own lack
of judgment in the matter on that. But what was the
point of having changed his name to something so
strong as, well, Dr. Strong, if it never got used? Still,
even Dr. Richard would be better than Dr. Richie, as if
he was some comic-book character.

"Maggie? Oh, yes, from the seminar." He shouldn't
really see her without an appointment. She might think
it was all right to drop in casually, and of course it wasn't.
Not if he wanted to look like a busy and important man.
But perhaps, just this once, it would be all right.

He liked Maggie. He considered her one of his success stories. Why, when she had started in the Bold and
Beautiful workshop she had been about as memorable
as a dishcloth hung over a faucet to dry.

But at his last seminar, the one where he had delivered the line "Go after what you want. Erase self-

doubt," he had noticed she looked quite stunning, her true feminine beauty shining through, a sparkle in her eye that had not been there before.

He had paraphrased that line from the daily install-ment of "Living Airy with Dr. Terry," which Richie taped faithfully and then watched with a black heart.

How dare that little fat man, who bore an appalling resemblance to a balding leprechaun, discuss weight loss when he obviously never intended to lose a pound himself?

Still, people adored the TV doctor and couldn't seem to get enough of him. Richard had seen Dr. Beachball doing guest segments on Larry King, and "Oprah" and "Saturday Night Live." There was talk of moving "Liv-ing Airy with Dr. Terry" to prime time.

Why was Dr. Terry getting what Richie deserved? Still, Dr. Terry did come up with memorable one-line exercises, and Richie had pilfered that one about eras-ing self-doubt. He'd delivered it with aplomb, but then lived in fear that someone would recognize it and call him on it, but no one had. After a while it started to feel as if maybe he had said it first.

Anyway, back to Maggie. That night after the semi-nar he had been in his office. He liked the idea of peo-ple walking by outside and noticing his light on. He felt it looked so good when people worked late, as if they were single-mindedly and passionately dedicated to their life work—which of course he was, so naturally he would want to look that way. But that night he had been watching yet another tape of Dr. Terry. It was not unlike doing research in his field, or consulting with a colleague, though Dr. Terry was more a showman than a real doctor. Richie liked to fill in the dull moments on the show—of which there were many he felt—by coming up with new names for Dr. Browell like Dr. Eatwell and Dr. Beachball.

But Richie, while fast-forwarding commercials, had glanced out the window, and he had seen a woman in a red dress getting out of her cute little gold Beetle in the parking lot shared by the hospital and his own clinic. He had nearly dropped the channel changer when he recognized her as Maggie Sullivan!

Naturally, he could make a little time in his day for such a success story, especially since she did look so fine in a red dress.

Would it be professional to invite her out for dinner?

The thought fled his mind when she came through the door. Oh, dear. His protégée had taken several giant steps backward.

Maggie was in a crumpled suit that looked like it had been rescued from the recycle bin. It was the unfortunate color of porridge.

She wore no makeup and it was obvious from the puffiness around her eyes that she had been crying.

"Miss Sullivan," he said in a soothing tone, "what can I do for you?"

"Oh, Dr. Richie," she said, and it all came out. About how she had been doing the homework and trying so hard to be bold, and how she had met a man.

And he had betrayed her.

Dr. Richie looked at the pain in her face and was taken aback at how heartbreak transformed her from the beautiful woman he had seen a few nights ago...to this.

He felt an unfamiliar ache in his own chest.

Guilt?

How many times had he done this to a woman who had given her heart to him? Too many to count. The thought shamed him, and he was really not a man accustomed to shame.

There was one woman in particular, and suddenly he could feel the softness of her eyes on him, the way he had felt when he was with her.

So long ago…the damage he had done was way too much to ever repair.

But, he thought, unused to thinking esoterically, so a bit surprised by himself, perhaps people were allowed to make amends with someone other than the one they had done the actual damage to.

He didn't know if he could repair Maggie's world. But he did know there was a man out there who was walking away from a really good woman. One of those rare women—so deep and sincere, so true, that their love could haunt you forever.

Could he use his own experience to help another man off the empty road he himself had chosen? And help Maggie at the same time?

"What did you say your chap's name is?" he asked.

"Does it matter?" Maggie asked.

"Yes, it does, my dear. Yes, it does."

The very next day Richard drove to the construction site of Luke August. He had gotten a work address from the hospital files.

He was feeling very pleased with himself, like Robin Hood, out doing his good deed for the day. He was dressed in a lovely gray Armani suit that made him look extremely successful and that commanded respect. He drove up to the site in his Cadillac, a small symbol of his status that he had treated himself to on his appointment as Chief of Staff.

Unfortunately, he got out of the car into a mud puddle.

And things went downhill from there. No one came out from the job to see what he wanted, and so after a few minutes he was forced to pick his way gingerly through the mud.

"I'm looking for Luke August," he said to the first man he encountered.

The man, unshaven and dirty from head to foot and wearing a T-shirt that said "Pick a Stud, Pick a Carpenter" nodded curtly to another man.

Dr. Richard looked at the man who had been pointed out to him and felt a moment's doubt. Somehow Luke August was not what he'd expected. The man was as big as a mountain, physically strong, toughness in every line of his face.

He was one of those men who radiated absolute confidence in himself, who wouldn't watch a program called "Living Airy with Dr. Terry" if his life depended on it, nor would he sign up for a seminar called Bold and Beautiful, either.

"Mr. August?"

The man fastened his eyes on him. They were astonishingly green and snapping with impatience.

Dr. Richard could see why he would appeal to women, and felt a little finger of annoyance, or maybe it was jealousy.

Only one woman had ever found him attractive before he put the title Doctor in front of his name. After that it was different, of course.

"Yeah?" August said rudely, as if Dr. Richard Strong was a bothersome flea, a salesman or an insurance broker.

"I need a word with you privately. I'm a doctor."

The man's expression changed. His brow furrowed. "I didn't think doctors made house calls anymore. Something come back on one of those tests?"

Dr. Richard felt surprisingly nervous in the other man's presence. He realized he shouldn't have left his home territory, where he was the big man on campus, and everyone knew it and acted accordingly. "Actually, I'm here about Maggie Sullivan."

The man was on him in a second. Dr. Richie felt his shoulders pinned in a grip that was frighteningly powerful.

"Has something happened to Maggie? Is she all right?"

"She's fine," he said hurriedly to buy the release of his shoulders, which it did. "I mean, she's physically fine. I'm a psychologist. I'm the director of the Healthy Living Clinic."

"Oh, not a real doctor," Luke said with what sounded suspiciously like relief.

Richard wasn't quite sure how to handle the insult of that statement, so he forged ahead. "Maggie takes a seminar from me. It's called The New You: Bold and Beautiful."

If the man mountain in front of him had ever heard of it, he didn't appear impressed.

"I gave a homework assignment, Mr. August." He could feel himself getting flustered. For one thing, from Luke's reaction when he had thought Maggie was hurt, Richie was almost positive the man had real feelings for Maggie. Could you feel like that and have another woman on the go at the same time?

Richard blurted out why he had come in a disjointed statement that showed none of his normal poise as a speaker.

He finished with, "I've regretted it all my life, leaving that woman. Learn from my mistakes, Mr. August."

Luke August looked faintly amused and not the least as if he intended to learn from anyone's mistakes except his own.

Richard was furious that he had wasted his time on the man and shown his most vulnerable side. He felt foolish and somewhat less than the man who stood before him.

"Of course," he said haughtily, "if you plan to let her go, I may ask her out myself."

Something tightened in the man's face, and the muscle along the strong line of his jaw jerked. Richard could not help but notice the almost unconscious flex of the man's sculpted biceps as he squeezed the huge hammer in his hand.

"Good day," Richard said, and without waiting for a reaction, he scurried away from the piercing light in those green eyes, got in his Cadillac and drove away, certain he had made an enormous mistake.

What had he been thinking, spilling his guts, his secrets to a stranger? It had been a stupid thing to do, an error in judgment.

And yet, despite the lack of reaction, of any kind of empathy from the other man, Richard had to admit his burden, the one he had been carrying for so many years, felt lighter.

"Just don't do it again," he warned himself. It was the type of emotionally motivated hogwash that Dr. Eatwell would approve of.

Would he really ever ask Maggie out? He thought of the way she had looked in that red dress and felt his mouth go dry and his good sense go out the window.

Seven

"Somebody else want a house built?" Brian asked Luke.

"Yeah. I told him I was too busy." Luke watched the Caddie pull out of the mud puddle it had been parked in and drive away. He managed, just barely, not to throw his hammer at the departing vehicle.

"Too bad. It looked like he had some bucks."

And didn't women just love that? The big bucks, the big cars, the big fancy offices, the title.

"He's a doctor," Luke offered up grudgingly. Maggie didn't seem like the type who would be overly impressed with that kind of stuff. Did she?

"Somebody you met at the hospital?"

"No, a friend sent him."

A friend? Whoo boy. That didn't begin to describe his complicated relationship with Maggie, not that Brian needed to know the details.

That doctor had seemed to Luke to be a bit of a flake. Why was Maggie taking seminars from him? She didn't seem like a person who needed any help with her life. The big question, of course, if Doctor Dweeb asked her out, would she say yes?

The thought of Maggie playing pool at Morgan's Pub with that man made Luke feel unaccountably angry. Not that the good doctor would take her to play pool.

Probably the opera or a fancy dinner or both. Isn't that what Maggie deserved? No! There had been something very off-putting about that guy, and nothing about his story of heartbreak and regret had inspired Luke to trust him even a little bit.

And how insulting was it that he, Luke, had been Maggie's homework assignment?

He stopped himself short. He had to look at this another way, before he tracked down that Caddie and its driver and did some serious damage.

And the other way of looking at it was this: he had gone out with Maggie Sullivan twice. He had known her five days—and she'd consulted a head doctor about it? Luke August had done as much damage to Maggie's sweet little life as he intended to do.

He'd let her go, and he wasn't looking back! And yet for the rest of the day he had the uneasy feeling he was punishing himself for that decision, or at least trying to outrun the feeling of regret that tried to take over his mind. Luke ignored his injuries and pulled out all stops on the house he was building. Long after Brian had called it a day, until the summer light was fading from the sky, Luke nailed and lifted and tore apart, hoping to exhaust himself.

It didn't work. When he finally climbed into bed, he

was aware of his aching back, the oppressive heat in his room, and the oppressive direction his mind wanted to take. Unwillingly he recalled the moments before Dr. Strong had revealed he had designs on Maggie.

In that moment when Dr. Strong had first introduced himself, before Luke had any idea of his business, Luke had experienced a shattering moment of fear. He had thought that for the doctor to have personally tracked him down to his job site, something must be terribly and urgently wrong with the latest round of tests Luke had undergone at the hospital.

For a man who had flirted with death often, Luke was not even remotely acquainted with fear. Where most people felt panic, he felt only a rush, the blissful euphoria of testing the boundaries of earth and emerging a victor. For all the times he had looked into the yawning abyss of death, Luke had never had a moment where his life had flashed before his eyes.

Not that his life had flashed before his eyes in those seconds before Dr. Strong had clarified his business. No, it was more as if he, Luke, had been given a moment of crystal-clear clarity. And in that moment he felt he had thrown his life away, that he had not done one thing of meaningful or lasting importance.

That moment of spiritual desolation paled in comparison to the moment when Luke's concern shifted to Maggie.

If something had happened to her, Luke had known in that instant, it would have felt as though his world, the whole world, had become a desert, with no oasis and no hope of an oasis.

If he felt that way, why had he told her the one lie

that was guaranteed to keep her away from him? He admitted the truth to himself. Feeling that way, so connected to her, so concerned about her, was twice as scary as leaping small chasms on motorcycles.

But in the final analysis, Luke knew he had done the right thing by breaking it off with Maggie and doing it in terms that made him look like the world's worst jerk to her.

Because if she had come back one more time, he would not have had the strength to resist her.

And the fact that after seeing her twice he had hurt her so deeply that she had to consult with the weird doctor meant that he was just not the kind of guy for her.

"Something you always knew," he reminded himself restlessly.

He gave up on trying to sleep and prowled out to his kitchen. Amber was still facedown on the table where he had left her. Hesitating, he turned her over.

He hoped their fight was over.

And it was. But not in the way he wanted. His relationship with Amber was terminated. He could see so clearly what he had done. His infatuation with a photograph had been the most immature of attempts to keep himself safe from any chance of real intimacy, from any chance of being hurt.

Luke August had made himself invulnerable to love's arrows.

"You say that as if it's a bad thing," he told himself. But that feeling he'd had when he'd thought, for seconds before the doctor had told him the real reason for his visit, that his life might be coming to an end was still fresh enough that he knew it was a bad thing to have made himself invulnerable.

He might have missed out on what was most important in life. And it wasn't seeing whether a motorcycle
designed for a top speed of ninety miles an hour could
do one hundred and ten.

In his bumbling way the doctor had probably accomplished something after all—he'd given Luke a wake-
up call.

Savagely, Luke tore off Amber's page in the calendar. With one more hard look, of regret and self-disgust,
he crumpled up the page she was on and stuffed her in
the garbage. Then he realized that might be a mistake.

Even questioning himself on such a simple decision
let Luke know he was on a slippery slope that he didn't
want to be on. He had never been a man who questioned
himself. He made decisions quickly and decisively and
he didn't look back.

Of course, that did explain seven trips to the hospital in five years.

So, he wasn't quite ready to dispose of Amber yet.
He had planned to see Billy soon. Why not take Amber
along? Find a new loving home for her with somebody
at exactly the right maturity level to enjoy her?

He plucked her out of the garbage, thankful real food
was rarely eaten here so the picture was still clean. He
did his best to erase the wrinkles from her picture with
his fist. Finally, he went back to bed. But he did not sleep.

Luke had always slept the deep sleep of a man who
pushed himself to his physical limits. Was this going to
be his life from now on? Wide-awake nights of tossing
and turning and thinking and questioning?

According to the doctor, a regret over the road not
taken could haunt for a long, long time. Maggie might

marry that doctor. Luke had given her nothing to hope for. He had no right to want to interfere in her life.

"You need to get on a motorcycle," Luke told himself. He looked at his bedside clock. It was Wednesday now, three in the morning. He had to work in a few hours. He had to have lunch with his mother. It was always best to be on full alert for lunch with her. But no amount of ordering, wishing or demanding could make him sleep.

And suddenly riding a big bike through an inky night seemed like just the remedy for the restlessness of his soul. He took his Harley and within minutes was on Interstate Number Five heading south to Salem. The road was nearly empty; he shared it only with big transport trucks and not that many of them. There were places where the road was long and straight and free of traffic. The ribbon of road seemed to meet the stars on the horizon. Instead of feeling sleepy, Luke felt more and more awake, and though no answers to the troubling dilemma of his life came to him, he felt a certain measure of peace.

At five, he used his cell phone to call Brian and tell him he wouldn't be in until later in the afternoon. He was never late. He rarely trusted anyone to look after the job site, not even Brian who was more than capable, and he could hear the pleasure in Brian's voice that he was being given this opportunity to show what he could do.

Luke turned the bike around, and rush-hour traffic was beginning as he hit the outskirts of Portland once more.

Luke was feeling much better by the time he arrived at the hospital. It was still very early when he got there. He crept through the halls, avoiding any encounter with Nurse Nightmare, not because it wasn't visiting hours, but because by now she might have heard—along with the head doc—how badly Luke had treated Maggie.

"Hey, kid," he whispered from the door. "You want to sneak out of here for a while?"

Billy turned and looked at him. "Luke!"

He looked at the light that went on in the boy's face. He felt unworthy of it. And at the same time it made him feel maybe his entire life hadn't been a meaningless screwup after all.

Luke put his finger to his lips. "I've got my motorcycle outside. Want to go for a ride around the block?"

"Your Harley?" Billy whispered. "One of my life dreams is to ride on a Harley."

Such a simple life dream. Maybe that was part of what was missing from Luke's life—dreams. Still, if he could give Billy a life dream, that was pretty cool.

While Billy found his street clothes, Luke went and donned Fred's uniform and found a gurney, put Billy on it, and then stacked folded linens and pillows around him.

Every time he said good morning to someone in his Fred voice, or asked someone to make way for the linen cart, he would watch the bedding tremble from Billy's concealed laughter.

Luke was sure he probably could have got a pass, now that he knew such a thing existed, but why bother? This was more fun.

At his favorite back door, they unloaded Billy, who was laughing so hard he was bent over double.

Luke brought him out to the parking lot. The boy touched the bike with the reverence of one who understood completely what this machine meant. Power. Speed. Freedom.

"It's an exact replica of the one used in the movie *Terminator*," Luke told Billy.

"Wow," Billy said on a breath, needing no more explanation. Luke doubted if Maggie would know what *Terminator* was. But he wasn't thinking of Maggie anymore, he reminded himself sternly.

Luke showed Billy how to strap on the helmet, and they were off. He had planned on a short trip, but when Billy yelled with pure delight and threw both his arms open wide to embrace the wind, somehow it just ended up differently. Luke realized he wasn't going to be just late. He wasn't going to make it to work today at all. He followed the Willamette River to Scappoose. They stopped and had breakfast there, Billy chattering away with excitement, eating more food than Luke had ever seen him eat.

Still, Luke noticed a tired pallor beginning to overtake the joy that shone in Billy's eyes, so instead of going on after breakfast he turned around and headed for home.

"One of my favorite rides is a huge loop," he told Billy when they were back at the hospital. "I follow the Columbia up to the coast, through Astoria and come back along the ocean for thirty or forty miles before I return to Portland. It's a day trip. And it's great. When you get out of here, you and I are doing it."

"Really?"

Luke nodded, again humbled by the look on the boy's face, hope and hero worship mingled in embarrassing proportions.

"I got something else for you, too." He took Amber

from the inside pocket of his leather jacket. "This is a reminder of today."

Billy's eyes were nearly popping out of his head when he opened the folded piece of calendar paper. "She's hot," he said hoarsely.

"Yeah, she was my roommate for a long time, but you can have her now."

"Wow."

"That's a '94 Harley Davidson Fatboy she's leaning over, just like mine."

Billy was obviously just too tired for the whole backdoor thing, so Luke brought him through the front. The ward was in chaos, until Billy was spotted, and then he was surrounded by people who were so glad to see him.

"I just went for a motorcycle ride," he said importantly. "On a Harley Fathead with my friend Luke."

Luke didn't correct him about the proper name for the bike. He folded his arms across his chest, and then noticed a presence beside him.

"I don't suppose you could have let us know Billy was going on an outing," Nurse Nightmare said through pursed lips.

"I will next time. I promise."

"He looks very happy," she said, and Luke heard the tiniest note of approval in her voice. "Mr. August, sometimes I think there might be hope for you."

That meant she hadn't found out he had ditched Maggie yet. He thought he'd better leave on a good note, and that meant before Billy posted Amber in his room.

Still, he asked the question he had been afraid to ask all this time. He took a deep breath and braced himself for the worst possible answer. "Is Billy going to die?"

The words sounded so stark and so real. And while the question made his own problems seem puny, it also reminded him of mortality and time limits, of things left undone, of experiences not had, of the road not taken.

"Of course," Nurse Nightmare said, so matter-of-factly that Luke wanted to choke her. But then she went on. "Mr. August, Billy is going to die and so are you and I. It's the wrong question. The right question is *how* are we all going to live? Today? This moment? Billy needs to seize his moments, but so do you and I."

Luke blew out a breath. What was it about him lately? Why was he attracting all this advice about how to live his life?

Why was he seeing people in a different light? For instance, when he cast a sideways glance at Nurse Nightmare, today he did not see a battle-ax. It was true she was no beauty and had aged gracelessly, but Luke saw a woman who had chosen to give her life to a very hard vocation, and who had made her peace with it, been open to the lessons it taught her.

Could he say the same?

"You're a wise woman, Nurse Wagner."

"I didn't know you knew my name," she said. "I understand you call me Nurse Nightmare."

"The mistake was mine. And I meant it about you being wise."

"Oh, pooh. I'm just repeating what I've heard. Haven't you ever watched 'Living Airy with Dr. Terry'?"

"Good God, no."

"You should."

"What does that mean, Living Airy?" he said doubtfully.

"I interpret it as meaning living with lightness and joy."

He didn't want to tell her if that was her goal, she had forgotten to pass it on to her face. Instead he said, "Is he anything like Dr. Strong?"

She sniffed. "Imitation is the poorest form of admiration."

He thought he'd leave her on that cheerful note. He checked his watch. He was a lucky man. He could just make lunch with his mother.

She was fifteen minutes late. She walked in, still beautiful despite her nearly sixty years. Of course, she had access to a good plastic man and wasn't afraid to use him.

She was way overdressed for Marcy's and didn't have a clue, picking her way through the tight tables on impossible heels. *The* earrings, her last gift from his father before he had passed, dripped from her ears. The suit was pink and looked like it was made of some kind of soft fur.

He got up when she came to his table and kissed her on both cheeks, European style.

"This place is…cute," she said uncertainly.

"Good food. Mom, it's July, aren't you hot in that getup?"

"It's angora," she said with pleasure as if that made it worth the trouble.

"And those earrings. You shouldn't wear them without a bodyguard."

"Nonsense. No one would ever think they were real."

That was his mother's logic in a nutshell.

"So, do you have holes in your hands? From making concrete yesterday?"

"Pouring," he corrected her, and yet still felt a small bit of surprise. There had been a time when she wouldn't have had any idea what he'd said to her an hour after a conversation.

Of course, since he'd pretty much given up talking to her, she probably listened more carefully.

No, it was more than that. His mother actually looked good. None of that discontent radiating from her as it had done in his childhood. Her eyes had always been restless, skipping here and there, always looking for something more interesting than what was right in front of her. Today her eyes were steady and serene.

"No, no holes." He held up his hands for inspection. "I wore gloves."

"Good for you. I hope this means you're going to start looking after yourself. It's distressing how you're always hurting yourself. I know it's my fault. It's the only time you ever got attention when you were young. I'm sorry, Luke."

"Mom, you've got to quit apologizing for how it was. It embarrasses me and it can't change anything."

"I just want to own my part in it. I was a dreadful mother."

"Hey, I was fed and clothed. I don't recall ever being beaten."

"By me," she said softly. "You found a way to beat yourself, didn't you?"

"Stop it, for Pete's sake," he said desperately.

"I just want to say one more thing, and then I will never mention it again, Luke, if it makes you uncomfortable. I promise."

It sounded like an okay trade-off, not that her promises had ever been worth anything, but he rocked his chair back and folded his arms over his chest and listened.

"I drank too much. So did your father. We cared about appearances. We cared about achieving. We cared about how we looked. All because we couldn't care about anything real. The more everything inside me was falling apart, the more I tried to fix everything outside of me to look perfect.

"And you kept defying me by refusing to be a perfect child, by reminding me that the outside world I was so busy creating was such a lie. You kept reminding me I would never be in control of the world, and least of all you. You kept trying to show our poor, pathetic family something was drastically wrong.

"I missed every single thing that was important," she said softly. "I had the maids and the swimming pool and the house and the memberships.

"But I don't know what happened to the first tooth you lost. I missed the time you played Fonzie in the school rendition of *Happy Days*. I missed your cries for help and love and attention. I missed every single thing that was important. I was entrusted with the care of the most beautiful and wondrous miracle in the whole world—a small boy—and I was not worthy of it. And for that I am truly, truly sorry."

"Okay," he said uncomfortably and let his chair drop back down. "Now it's over, right? The shrimp special looks pretty good. Or the steak."

It was too much to hope that it was over, of course.

"I just want you to know, Luke, that I am very proud of the man you have become despite the obstacles put in your way. I see you as strong and successful and independent, and that says quite a lot about your character that you would become those things, given the lack of parental guidance and approval you had."

"Great. Let's order."

But her hand covered his. "I guess what makes me sad, Luke, is that I see how alone you are as a result of the lack of warmth and caring in the way you were raised. Once, you found a dog. It was a dreadful creature, but it loved you so sweetly and unconditionally, and I even took that away. It didn't fit in my perfect house."

"Stinkbomb," he said. "She really was stinky. I doubt if I'd allow her in my house now, either."

"Well, Luke, what do you allow in?"

He studied the menu intently, hoping she would get the hint. He didn't want to talk about this!

She went on softly, relentlessly, "Now I see how afraid you are to be intimate. I see your wariness, your lack of trust in the whole process of relationships."

"I'm not afraid of anything," he said. Wasn't that what he'd spent his whole life proving? That he was not afraid? But had he not looked this very fear in the face last night and blinked first?

"Yes, you are," his mother said softly. "You're afraid to take the greatest risk of all."

He wanted to challenge her. He wanted to say, *And what would that be?*

But he knew she would tell him. And he knew she would be right.

"What about Amber?" he said. "That's a relationship." He wondered what corner of hell was reserved for men who lied to their mothers, even if it was in self-defense.

His mother looked at him shrewdly. "I may have been a lousy mother, Luke, but I could still always tell when you were lying."

"I think I'll have the shrimp," he decided, looking at the menu. "How about you, Ma?"

It had always ticked her off royally to be called Ma, so of course he had done it all the more often.

But when the waiter came, she set down her menu and said, "Ma will have the shrimp, too, please."

And for the first time Luke understood it was real. His mother was really changing. And she was trying so hard to bring him with her.

And it was just too damn late. Wasn't it?

In the span of less than two days, three different people had told him, in different ways that it was time to take a good hard look at his life and decide what was really worth having.

It was a message from the universe, and he didn't have to watch "Living Airy with Dr. Terry" to know it.

But that didn't mean he had to do anything about it. And he was not at all sure that he would.

"Hi, Billy," Maggie said softly from the doorway. Billy was kneeling on his bed, taping something to the wall above it.

When he turned and looked at her, Maggie noticed he was pale and tired, but even more noticeable was the sparkle in his eyes and the welcoming grin.

She was pleased with herself. Obviously allowing him to deal with some of the issues he was having about his illness was a great help to him.

"Luke took me out on his motorbike today," he

said. "We went to Scappoose for breakfast. It was so awesome."

So much for the idea she had had anything to do with the happy light shining in Billy's eyes! Still, how could she not be happy for the boy?

Luke must just have a gift for that—turning the light on in people.

"That was nice of him," she said, and she meant it, even though there was a little worm of envy in her.

Luke had never invited her to ride his motorcycle with him.

But of course he wouldn't have. That might have involved some sort of explanation to the girlfriend, or about the girlfriend, and it was very clear that he was a man who didn't care for the complications of making explanations.

"Look what he gave me," Billy said, sitting back on his haunches to admire whatever he had just posted over his headboard.

Maggie stepped closer to the bed and peered at what Billy had just hung there.

It was an absolutely disgraceful picture of a girl posed suggestively over a monstrous piece of shining chrome, rubber and metal. Redheaded, the girl in the photo was exquisitely beautiful in an edgy way that complemented the black jacket she wore and the motorcycle she leaned over.

She was spilling out of the jacket, and her expression was warmly seductive.

"Luke gave that picture to you?" Maggie asked, trying not to let her disapproval be too overt.

"Yup. A souvenir of our ride today. That's the kind of motorcycle he has, a Harley Fathead. Just like the one in *Terminator*."

Billy's newfound expertise on motorcycles was demonstrated with a certain endearing pride.

"What is *Terminator?*" she asked him.

Billy groaned, and she found out quite a bit more about the movie than she wanted to know.

"So, the picture on your wall is simply about the motorbike. Neither you nor Luke even notice—" She leaned closer to the picture and squinted at the scrawled signature. "Amey?"

"Maggie, you can't be a guy and not notice her. She's gorgeous, isn't she?" Billy said it worshipfully.

Maggie managed to grunt, even as she registered that being in possession of the picture made Billy feel like one of the guys, an exclusive club she was fairly certain he had not felt included in in the past.

She wondered, as she had before, if there was more to Luke than met the eye.

"Her name's not Amey. It's Amber."

"I see," Maggie said and then frowned. Amber? Wasn't that an odd coincidence? That was a name Maggie was never going to be able to forget, or hear without cringing!

Billy chuckled as if he was now a major player in a private male club.

"Luke said she used to be his roommate, but now she's all mine."

Maggie tried to digest this information.

"Are you saying Luke shares accommodations with the woman who modeled for this picture?"

Billy looked at her, baffled. "I don't think so. Sheesh. Wouldn't that be something?"

"It would indeed," Maggie said a little tersely.

But it was all making sense now. He had said he was going home to his roommate, Amber. He had not ever said he had a girlfriend.

And when Maggie had tried to get the specifics out of him, how had he worded it?

As if she didn't have every word of that conversation committed to memory. Luke had said of Amber, "She hangs around." He had neglected a fairly crucial piece of information. Amber hung around, all right.

"On a wall," Maggie said.

"What?"

"Oh, nothing." She sat on the edge of Billy's bed. "So, tell me all about your adventure with Luke," she invited.

And without any prodding at all, Billy told her. In between sound effects and high drama, Maggie heard what was not being said in words. Luke was the man her heart had always told her he was.

She visited with Billy for a while longer. He gave her a sealed envelope with his private wishes in it before she left. Crossing the parking lot toward her Beetle, she saw a stream of people going into the Healthy Living Clinic. She realized there was a B&B seminar tonight. She had told Kristen she would not be attending, but that was before this new development.

She changed directions, slipped in the door and found an empty chair behind Kristen.

"He lied," she said, leaning forward in her chair, her lips almost on Kristen's ear.

Kristen jumped, and then twisted in her chair, and gave her a sympathetic look. "I know. You told me. The girlfriend. Snake."

"I mean he lied about the girlfriend. I don't think he has one at all."

Maggie felt the woman next to her elbow her gently in the ribs.

"Shhh," the same woman said to Kristen, bringing her finger sternly to her lips. Kristen, not near the people pleaser Maggie was, ignored the woman completely.

"No live-in lover?" she said.

"I don't think so."

At the mention of the lover, Maggie's neighbor's disapproval had turned to interest that was just a bit too avid. Maggie stood and nodded at the back door. Seconds later they were standing out in the hall by the coffee machine.

Maggie told her about going to see Billy and the horrible poster he had inherited.

"I think Amber the poster girl was the roommate he was referring to," she concluded.

"Are you sure that you aren't just seeing things as you want them to be, Maggie?" Kristen said gently. "You seem to have fallen pretty hard for this guy."

With a sudden lift of her eyebrow, Kristen flicked out her cell phone. "His number?"

Maggie wanted to pretend she didn't know it, but Kristen would know her well enough to know she had memorized it out of the phone book by now. She had also memorized his address. He lived in Boring, which Maggie would have thought was a hilarious irony, if she was laughing about anything these days.

Reluctantly, she gave the number to Kristen, who, with no reluctance at all, punched it into her cell phone. Maggie heard his deep voice answer, and felt that quiver of longing.

"Amber, please," Kristen said crisply. "No? Sorry, wrong number." She clicked off and studied her phone for a moment. "Nice voice. Kind of has that raspy edge. Gave me shivers in the nicest way."

"But why did he do that?" Maggie said. "Why did he tell me he has a roommate when he doesn't?"

"There's only one reason a guy would make something like that up," Kristen told her, an expert on matters masculine.

"And what is that?"

"Honey, are you sure you don't know?"

"No."

"Well, when you figure it out, let me know." Kristen was smiling at her with the dewy look she usually reserved for smarmy movies.

"You think he cares about me? So much he's scared himself?"

"I think."

"Kristen, he's gorgeous. You heard him. His voice gives women shivers. Wait until you see the whole package. He's not the kind of man who would ever go for a girl like me."

"Why can't you see what the rest of the world sees so clearly, Maggie? You are so beautiful. Oh, not like Britney or Shania. Heart beautiful. Genuine."

"Oh, let's go see what Dr. Richie is saying," Maggie suggested, embarrassed.

"I hope he has a dynamite homework assignment this time," Kristen said, holding open the door and letting Maggie go through ahead of her.

And he did. They took their seats just in time to hear the assignment.

"Take a risk," Dr. Richie encouraged them. "Not just any risk, take the greatest risk of your lives."

"Ooh," Kristen said approvingly, turning in her chair to wink at Maggie, "now that is what I call a perfect homework assignment."

After the class, Maggie was trying to scramble over bodies to get out of there, but Dr. Richie calling her name stopped her mid-flight.

"Miss Sullivan, could I have a moment?" When Maggie arrived at the front, the doctor looked at her warmly. "Maggie, I wanted to thank you for your trust in me the other day. I was deeply honored by it."

"Oh." She now found the fact she had turned to him embarrassing.

"You seem more yourself again tonight," he said warmly. "I watched you come in. Your step was lighter. That sparkle is back in your eyes."

Maggie was a little taken aback that anybody paid that much attention to her. She only hoped he hadn't noticed her and Kristen rudely yakking through much of his presentation.

"Is your personal life, er, back on track?"

"I don't know," she said. She supposed that would depend on how the homework assignment went.

"Well, good. I mean it's not good that you don't know if your personal life is back on track, but it is good that you're not dwelling on it."

She had done nothing but dwell on it!

"He's not worthy of you."

"How do you know?" Maggie asked.

Dr. Richie looked vaguely uncomfortable. "Just a guess," he said breezily. "Anyway, on to other things.

You know, tonight's homework was to take a risk, and what kind of leader would I be if I didn't follow my own advice?"

When Maggie didn't answer, he chuckled uncomfortably, fitted a finger between his necktie and his collar and gave a little tug.

"So, this is my risk," he said nervously. "Would you like to go out for dinner one night? And maybe to the opera after?"

Maggie stared at him, flabbergasted. A few months ago—no, even days ago—it would have seemed like an invitation from heaven.

Dr. Richie was handsome and articulate and successful.

And tonight all those qualities paled when she compared them to the qualities of another man.

A man who was afraid to love her.

A man who had given a young man with very little to hope for a day of carefree joy.

A man who took great risks all the time. But the greatest risk of all? Never.

"Dr. Richie," she said gently, "thank you for asking. I am deeply flattered. But no."

He looked stunned, as if he couldn't believe she had refused him, and she hurried away from him and out the door where Kristen was waiting with avid interest.

"What did he want?"

"He asked me out," Maggie said. Both she and Kristen turned when a woman hovering near the coffee table gasped audibly.

Maggie thought the woman's name was Carolyn or maybe Carrie but she wasn't quite sure. The woman was lovely, but very quiet. She kept to herself and didn't participate in the class at all.

Maggie saw she had knocked over a coffee cup, which would explain the gasp. She smiled sympathetically, and then returned her attention to Kristen.

"Seriously? Dr. Richie asked you out?"

"Unfortunately."

"Isn't that a bit unethical? I mean he's the leader of the class."

"I don't know, Kristen. He's a doctor but we're not his patients."

"You went to him for advice."

"I hardly think that makes me a client."

"I guess you're right," Kristen said, then shrugged. "So what's your risk going to be, Maggie?"

But Maggie wasn't telling anyone that. She was not even sure she had admitted it to herself yet.

"Oooh," Kristen said with wicked approval, just as if Maggie had said her most private thoughts out loud.

Eight

"Hi," Luke said. His eyes were a smoky shade of green, intent on her face. His voice was deep and low and welcoming. He leaned against the jamb of his outside door, his arms folded across his chest. His arms were gorgeous in the fading light, sleek and muscular. He was wearing a simple white T-shirt and dark blue denims that hung low off his hips.

In that simple greeting, Maggie's self-doubt was, finally, erased.

Maggie knew she had done the right thing by coming here, to that address she had memorized out of the phone book just as surely as she had the phone number.

And she knew also she had done the right thing by coming as she was—not in a porridge-colored pantsuit, and not in a red dress, but in the same comfy stretchy jeans she had worn to see Billy and to the seminar.

Tonight, she had come to him as herself.

"Hi," she said back.

As she went up the walkway toward the welcome in his eyes, she had a sensation of homecoming, as if they both could fight this thing as hard and as long as they wanted, but in the end they belonged together in some way she did not fully understand.

"What took you so long?" he asked when she stood before him. He lifted a lock of her hair, and she tilted her chin to look up into his eyes.

She wondered what had taken her so long to figure it out. Self-doubt she supposed. "You mean to figure out that Amber was fictitious?"

He shook his head. "No. To get here from wherever you were."

"You couldn't have been expecting me," she sputtered. "This is a surprise."

"I've been waiting for you ever since I got the call asking for Amber. Not your voice. A friend?"

"Not my idea to call," she said. "Yes, a friend."

"I could have said she was here, you know."

"Why didn't you?"

"I like to live dangerously?"

She stared him down.

"Okay. I'm done playing games. What made you guess there was no Amber?"

"You left a clue with Billy. She's hanging out in his room now. Literally hanging out—of her jacket."

He sighed. "I miss her."

Maggie thumped him on the arm. "You do not, you liar."

"You better think of that before you walk through this

door, Maggie Mouse. I'm a pathological liar, and that is probably the least of my faults."

Her breath caught in her throat. So, the risk had paid off. He was not sending her away. He was inviting her in. He wanted her to be here as much as she wanted to be here. He was giving her the option of running, but still inviting her in.

"Your house isn't what I expected," she told him, delaying. She liked it out here on his front stoop. She liked the way he looked and she liked this house, and she didn't want to rush anything. She wanted to savor each small detail of this encounter.

He lifted a dark slash of eyebrow at her. "No? What did you expect?"

"A bachelor pad at one of those complexes with a pool and party room."

"Ah. The kind of digs that go well with pathological liars."

"Exactly."

It felt light and easy between them, as if nothing had ever gone wrong, and as if nothing ever could.

"Who would have expected Luke August to live in Boring?"

"Nobody," he said. "That's why I live here. Nothing predictable about me. So, are you coming in, Maggie Mouse?"

"Depends what you have planned, Luke Louse."

He laughed and held open the screen for her. "I deserved that. And I have no agenda. I was watching a ball game and planning to make some popcorn."

"My idea of a good time," she said, and meant it. "I love baseball."

He shot her a swift sidelong look. "You're kidding, right?"

"Nope."

"The woman of my dreams," he muttered.

She could only hope. The inside of the house was as surprising as the outside. She was not sure what she had expected—some sign, she supposed, of a lifestyle in keeping with a great-looking single guy.

Instead, the house was plain and neat. There was no black leather and chrome, no dimmer switches on the lights, no expensive stereo system.

A huge TV was the predominant piece of furniture in his living room. It was on, the Angels up to bat in the bottom of the ninth. There was a couch that looked as if it had never been sat on, and a recliner chair that was worn nearly right through its leather covering.

"You want some popcorn?" he asked. "And a soda?"

"Yes." She followed him through to his kitchen. Again, everything was neat and tidy, but devoid of feminine touches.

Not only was Amber not in residence, unless she was mistaken this had been a male sanctuary for a long, long time.

The strangest thing was that Maggie felt as though she should be uncomfortable. She was chasing a man who had spurned her. She was bearding the lion in his den.

And yet, as she took the popcorn from him, and laughed as he liberally poured the melted butter on it, she was aware of feeling comfortable, her sensation of homecoming deepening.

He carried the popcorn through to the living room,

she the soda. A moment later they were sitting shoulder to shoulder on his couch.

"Don't worry about the butter, Maggie Mouse."

"I wasn't going to. Did you see that catch in centerfield?"

They laughed and talked and exchanged baseball info as the game wound down. Then it was over. The popcorn was gone, and so were the drinks. It was a weeknight and she knew it would be sensible to go.

But, frankly, she was tired of always being sensible.

Luke, of course, was probably rarely sensible. "So," he said, settling his back onto the arm of the sofa and stretching his legs out so that his toes tickled her thighs. "Tell me everything."

"Like?"

"Were you a brainiac in school?"

"I'm afraid so, yes." It was quite hard to focus with his toes playing chopsticks on her pant leg. "Chess club, debate team. No date for the prom."

"Boys at that age are very shallow."

"They change?"

"Yes!"

"I'd believe you if I hadn't seen Amber firsthand."

He had the grace to grin a bit sheepishly. "I bet you had a pet goldfish."

"Three of them. And you had the dog that disappeared."

"Yeah. Do you think that has something to do with me not wanting to get close to people? My mother thinks so. I had lunch with her today."

Now, who would have ever imagined Luke was the kind of guy who had lunch with his mother? In a flash the conversation had gone from lighthearted to serious, and she felt him reaching out to her, trusting her.

"I do think you might have a few trust issues."

"You can still run, Maggie." His toes had stopped moving.

She picked up his foot and set it in her lap. She stripped off the sock and ran her hand over the tenderness of his instep.

"Maggie, don't do that. I haven't had a wink of sleep for twenty-four hours, and if I get any more relaxed, I'm a goner." Unless she was mistaken, Luke August's eyes were very heavy.

"I have a few trust issues of my own," she admitted, gently kneading the bottom of his foot with her knuckles.

"Yeah, I heard." His words were ever so slightly slurred with sleepiness.

"What?" she gasped.

"Hospital gossip. Sorry, sweetie. I know all about your sordid past."

"Like what?"

"I know you got left standing at the church."

"Oh!"

"Don't say it like that, as if it has anything to do with you. Because it doesn't. It was all about him. And just for your information, if I ever see him, I'm going to rearrange his face."

She laughed unsteadily. "You don't even know his name."

"Yes, I do." His eyes were closed now, his foot totally relaxed in her lap. And yet there was no mistaking the absolute danger in what he was saying.

A man talking about rearranging another man's face was totally barbaric, if you thought about it logically. But Maggie did not feel the least logical. In fact, Luke's protectiveness of her struck her as being very romantic.

"You want to tell me about him?" he asked. Again, she heard the faint slur of a very, very tired man.

"I don't think so," she said softly. Darnel seemed like something that had happened to another person, on another planet, in another time. All she felt toward Darnel at the moment was extreme gratitude—that some instinct in him had warned him not to settle, had warned him something was missing.

He had left her in an awkward position, but not nearly as awkward as it would have been if she met someone who made her heart sing as Luke did and she had already said "I do" to the wrong man.

"Okay. Then tell me everything else. Your favorite song, and your favorite flower, and your favorite movie." His voice was husky.

"Okay." She told him. His eyes remained closed, as if he was listening with intent enjoyment.

But as she was describing her favorite scene from *Shakespeare In Love,* a very gentle sound escaped from his lips. Stunned, she stared at him. Sure enough, his chest was rising and falling with deep regularity.

Had he gone to sleep?

"Luke?" she said tentatively.

He sputtered, and his hand reached for hers. She let go of his foot and reached back. When she took his hand, he tugged her into the wall of his chest. Wrapping his arms solidly around her, he buried his nose in her hair, sighed and snored.

She lay there, stiffly, in the circle of his arms.

This could only happen to her! She'd put the man of her dreams to sleep. It was horrible. It was insulting.

It was the story of her life.

But was there another way of looking at it? Luke was completely at ease with her. He trusted her. And given he was a man with a few trust issues, that might be every bit as important as passion.

Still, if she had an ounce of pride, she would get up and leave. But if her choice was between being proud and alone, or humble and with him, she was taking humble.

She relaxed. She placed her cheek on his chest, and her hand on the hollow of his stomach. She remembered, from once before when they had lain on top of each other, the solid and enticing strength of him.

She felt the steady rise and fall of his breathing and she felt strangely contented. Her own eyes felt heavy. She would just close them for a moment, and then she would find a blanket and cover him, tiptoe out the door and lock it behind her.

But somehow, perhaps because his hand found her hair and stroked it absently and dreamily, she never did get back up.

Luke woke at first light, felt the sweet weight of Maggie curled into him.

He'd fallen asleep on her! He couldn't believe it. It was probably a sign of aging and too many injuries.

But he *had* been up for more than twenty-four hours

CARA COLTER 179

without sleeping when she had showed up at his door. In his weakened state he had been happy to see her. In his weakened state he had been unable to send her away.

But now he'd had sleep, and he still felt weakened—by the nearness of her, by her softness and her scent.

She looked like hell, her hair messed, her light makeup smudged, her mouth agape, her clothes crumpled.

She looked adorable.

And like she was going to have one hell of a kink in her neck when she woke up.

He lifted her. She stirred but did not wake, and her weight in his arms was sweet and warm. She snuggled deeper into him, and he made his way down the hallway to his bedroom. He laid her gently between the sheets of his unmade bed and gazed down at her.

There had never been a woman in this bed. Or this house. He gazed at her for a moment longer, and then realized he felt sticky and rumpled. He grabbed a pair of gym shorts out of his bureau, changed, went into the kitchen and picked up the phone.

There was a square on the wall, where Amber used to be, that was darker than the rest of the wall.

"Should have used acrylic," he said.

"Acrylic?" Brian asked, amazed.

"Uh, sorry, partner. I'm not going to be in again today. Are you managing all right?"

"Yeah, fine, but are you okay? Is everything okay?"

"Never better."

"It's a girl," Brian said dryly. "I just knew it."

Luke went back to the bedroom, pulled back the comforter on the other side of the bed and slid in.

He turned on his side so he could look at her, lifted

the richness of her hair and sifted it through his fingers. He sighed and pulled her body into his.

And then he slept.

Luke was startled awake by a feminine cry, high and panicked, way too close to his ear. Cautiously, he opened one eye.

He was never going to figure Maggie Mouse out. Somehow, he might as well just resign himself to that fact. He had thought she might be pleased to see him first thing in the morning.

Despite being woken by a shriek to the look of dazed panic on her face, he still felt pleasure waking up beside her. Which, given that none of the normal things had transpired between them, he found rather astonishing.

Maggie's eyes skittered over him, then skittered away. She shut them tight, then opened them again as if she hoped to see a different set of scenery on her second try. When she didn't, another little mouselike squeak came from her.

"Hey," he said, "it's okay. It's me."

"I know it's you," she said. "I'm not sure that makes it okay."

She pulled the blanket up to her chin, had a second thought and peeped cautiously under it.

"Fully clothed," he told her dryly.

"I am. But you don't appear to be."

He was amazed, and just a little pleased she had noticed that in her quick glimpse under the blankets.

"In deference to your unexpected presence in my bed, I do have on a pair of shorts."

She blushed crimson.

"Not that kind," he said patiently. "Running shorts."

"It's the unexpected part that I'd like you to expand on," she said primly, as if his short attire was of no interest to her whatsoever. She had no idea how transparent she was. He had seen that she was mightily relieved about his clothing.

"I usually sleep nude," he informed her just to watch the crimson on her face deepen. He leaned up on one elbow to get a better look at the phenomenon.

"Just tell me, what am I doing in your bedroom, in your bed?"

Though it would have been fun to string her along to the point of near hysteria, he decided to put her out of her misery.

"We fell asleep on the couch. I woke up and noticed you were getting a crook in your neck, so I carried you in here."

"Is there a Boy Scout badge for that?" she asked suspiciously. "Was it your good deed for the day?"

"Yes, ma'am, that was my only motivation. A good deed for the, er, night."

"I'm not the kind of girl men scoop up in their arms and carry around!"

He thought that was a crying shame, a situation he might have to rectify. She apparently had no concept of how sexy men found the Me Tarzan, You Jane scenario. From the look of prim remoteness on her face she had quite a bit to learn in the sexy department.

It occurred to him that he was contemplating being the one to teach her, and the thought made his throat and mouth go dry as sandpaper. "Well, you were exactly that kind of girl last night."

"And your presence beside me is explained how?"

"One bed," he said. "And I am recovering from a back injury. One night on that couch and it probably would have been back to the hospital for me. I crawled in beside you. It was nice."

"What was nice?" she asked suspiciously.

"Lying down beside you."

"And that's all?"

"Maggie Mouse, you know how to insult a man! If there had been more than that, don't you think you'd remember?"

She smiled, a wobbly smile. "I suppose. I've just been acting strange lately. A stranger to myself. I can't always predict what's going to happen next. I mean the last thing I would have ever predicted was this. Waking up with you."

Luke laughed. "In my world, I'd call not knowing what happens next a good thing."

He looked at her lips, at her sleep-tousled hair, at the hazel of her eyes, at the swell of her breasts beneath the blanket.

He knew exactly what was supposed to happen next.

With anyone but Maggie.

She leaped from the bed. "I'm going to be late for work. I have to go home and shower. I have to change. Look at my clothes!"

He was looking at them. They were adorably rumpled. Her blouse was binding across her breasts.

"Call in," he suggested. "Tell them you won't be in today."

Her eyes went very round, as if he'd asked her to help him hide a bag of money with a bank emblem on the sack.

"I have never done that," she said, "not unless I was sick."

"Me, either. Or at least rarely. But I called in this morning and said I wouldn't be on the job site today."

"Really? Why?"

"It's time for us to get to know each other better, Maggie. I want to spend the day with you. Come on, play hooky with me. It's a gorgeous summer day."

She took a deep breath. She looked everywhere but at him.

He got out of bed and padded over to her. He took her chin between his fingers. "Please?" he said.

She looked him full in the face, her eyes bright with the longing just to say yes.

"What is your idea of getting to know a person?" she said. Her eyes moved uncomfortably to the bed and back to his naked chest.

From the way she licked her lips nervously Luke was pretty sure she liked his naked chest a whole lot. He flexed his biceps for her and her eyes fastened on it with fascination that was both innocent and intrigued.

This hardly seemed like the same woman who had attacked him in the front seat of her Volkswagen a few short days ago. Naturally, he thought that would be a wonderful way to get to know her, their lips and limbs tangled in the most erotic ways.

On the other hand, he'd gotten to know women like that before. It was a bit like putting the cart before the horse.

He wanted to know Maggie. He was astounded to find he wanted to do things right, to obey the rules.

That was a brand-new one for him. He wasn't sure he knew what the rules were.

But he was pretty sure if he followed Nurse Nightmare's advice and just required more of himself, he'd do all right.

"I was thinking we could pack a picnic and go to one of my favorite places in the country."

Her eyes told him he'd gotten it right. That he had somehow managed to be romantic. By God, it was true. He was romancing Maggie Mouse, and enjoying it immensely, too.

"Oh, Luke, that does sound wonderful. I'll call the office and rearrange some of my appointments. And then I'll go home and shower and change. I could be back here in, say, an hour?"

He found himself not wanting to let her go, not even for the hour it would take her to go and change and clean up.

That was a totally different experience for him. Usually when he woke up beside a woman, he couldn't wait to get rid of her.

But if Maggie left, she might come to her senses and never come back.

"Why don't you just grab a shower here, and I'll lend you something to wear? It's not as if we're going to the governor's ball."

"You'll lend me something to wear?" she asked doubtfully. "You don't have women's clothing here, do you?"

"Maggie, that would just be plain weird. Trust me."

Half an hour later he regretted his suggestion. Maggie emerged from the shower with a pair of his jeans on, cinched at the waist with a belt, rolled up at the cuffs. She had on one of his shirts, and it fit her so differently than him, hugging her curves. The irony was that the men's clothing was making her look erotically and completely feminine. Her hair was wet and wild, and she combed the tangles out of it with her fingers. Even from here he could smell the fragrance of her.

He wasn't going to tell her, but Maggie in his clothing, with her hair hanging in wet ropes that were making the shirt somewhat see-through, put the sexiness of that red dress she had worn the other night to shame.

He had never wanted more just to sweep a woman off her feet and carry her, caveman-style, back to his bed.

He managed, he was not sure how, to restrain himself. He'd made a quick trip to the corner bakery while she showered, not trusting himself to be in the same house with her, thinking of that water pouring down over the creaminess of her skin. He'd picked up a few things for breakfast and lunch. Now, he left some bagels and strawberry-flavored cream cheese out for her while he had his own shower.

"Are you ready to meet my girlfriends?" he said when he emerged a short while later.

"And they're where? Locked in the cellar?"

"Close," he said. "The workshop."

Then he took her out to the shop and introduced her to his other three girls, the Harley, his Honda dirt bike and the wrecked street bike.

She looked at the wrecked bike for longer than the other two. She reached out and touched some of the twisted metal. When she looked back at him, her face was pained.

"The bike looks like this, and you survived?"

"I'm tougher than I look."

Still, he could tell she was a bit shaken, and so he hurriedly filled the saddle bags with lunch things, then strapped the helmet to her head. He rolled the big Harley out of the garage. It purred to life, and she hopped on behind him.

"Hold on to me tight," he said. Her arms went around him, and he gave the big machine a hit of gas. It leaped forward and she gave a little shriek and tightened her hold, locking her fingers around his waist, pressing her cheek into his shoulder blade. Her legs were tucked behind his legs, and he was not sure if it was his imagination or reality that wonderful warmth radiated from where those legs formed a sensuous V around the small of his back, and the line of his rear.

He was so aware of everything as they rode, as if he had been transported into a world that vibrated with life and color and texture such as he had never known before.

"Are you taking me to Multnomah Falls?" she asked over the roar of the engine when he turned off onto the historic Columbia River Highway.

The well-known falls were just outside a village known as Bridal Veil. Much as he liked her, he was not taking Maggie any place with a name like that!

"Better," he called back, and turned off the main highway that led to Bridal Veil.

But he was almost sorry he had a destination in mind, and when they arrived at the next turnoff he considered going straight. He did not know what the road ahead held, because he had never traveled it, but suddenly in the sparkling light of a summer morning spent with a beautiful woman, it felt as if it didn't matter what it held. It would all be an equal adventure.

That road felt like a metaphor for his life, which was

probably why he chose to turn off on the more familiar route after all.

Maggie got off the bike, undid the strap of the helmet and shook her hair free. She looked around, astounded.

"This is your idea of a romantic place in the country? Better than Multnomah Falls?"

"Who said anything about romantic?" he asked.

In fact, it was one of his favorite places in the country, a dirt bike track with full rental facilities.

"Trust me," he said with a wink.

Moments later he had introduced her to Leonard, the owner-operator of Skookum Leo's Revvin' Rides. She was completely outfitted with gloves and pads and good boots, and they were both fitted with dirt bikes.

Luke gave her her first lesson. By the time she had stalled the bike three times and moved less than fifty feet she was howling with laughter.

This was the way he had always dreamed of seeing her. So carefree, playful, without any inhibitions.

When it was apparent she had no aptitude for learning to ride the bike, despite how much fun she was having, he climbed on behind her, covered her hands with his and physically moved her through the motions of gas and brake and changing gears.

It was his turn to have fun later, as she bumped them experimentally along a little novice track, forcing him to hold on to her for dear life.

Unfortunately, once he had maneuvered her through the basics, she caught on quickly and wanted to do it herself.

"Hey, wait," he called as she took off, leaving him in a shower of dirt. He mounted his own bike—not nearly as responsive and powerful as the Honda he had in his workshop, but still a good machine—and chased after her. She showed an amazingly bold side, glancing behind at him with fiendish glee, maneuvering the bike so he couldn't get by her.

"Slow down," he yelled, but either she couldn't hear him over the roar of the engines, or she was going to be a hard woman to slow down once she had sped up.

Luke couldn't help but wonder how that particular trait was going to translate in other areas of her life, such as the bedroom. Not that he could allow his mind to wander there if he didn't intend to have another major motorcycle accident!

To stop her, he actually had to get off his bike, wait for her to come around the track and flag her over.

"What?" she said breathlessly. "Luke, this is so much fun. I just couldn't have imagined."

"I thought we'd break for lunch. You're getting a sunburned nose."

"You, too," she said. He noticed she was still somewhat reluctant as he led the way off the track and to a quiet little picnic area under the trees.

Because it was a weekday, they didn't even have to listen to the constant high-pitched drone of engines. They had the place to themselves.

A little creek ran by, and Maggie took her sandwich, rolled the pant legs up even higher, kicked off her rented boots and dangled her feet in the water.

He stared at her feet, mesmerized by the daintiness of them. He had a little thing for feet. Her toenails were painted bright pink, a part of her true nature hidden from the world inside her shoes.

She patted the spot beside her. "I'm not sure when I remember having so much fun. A long time ago, I guess. My dad brought us into the mountains from time to time, Mount Hood, Timberline Lodge. We played in the snow and tobogganed. I remember I laughed like that until my sides hurt."

Luke thought her life had become much too serious if the last time she had let go so completely was when she was a child. Still, he knew the perfect remedy for it—him!

"Didn't you know that's my motto?" He kicked off his boots, rolled off his socks and plunked his feet in the water. He acknowledged that maybe if he had a thing or two to teach her about having fun, she might have a thing or two to teach him about bliss. In all the times he had ridden here, he had never once thought to dip his hot feet in this tiny, gurgling creek.

"I didn't know you had a motto." She wiggled her toes.

"Well, I do, and that's it. Live life as if you were tobogganing."

She laughed and tossed her hair over her shoulder. "What a wonderful plan for today," she said.

They talked over lunch, and Luke could not remember ever being with anyone when the conversation had flowed this easily, switching from lightness and laughter to deep things and then back again.

Maggie was as multifaceted as a diamond. Amber had had one dimension, but Maggie had many. He was pretty sure it would take a man a lifetime to know Maggie.

"Ready to get back at it?" he asked. He leaned toward her, inviting a sweet little after-lunch kiss.

Apparently she now preferred motorcycles, because

she missed the gesture completely in her rush to pull her feet out of the creek. She buried them in his shirt to dry off. Temptation teased him, and won. He captured her foot and held tight when she tried to pull away.

"Don't tickle me," she pleaded. "I hate being tickled."

He was pretty sure that was because no one had ever tickled the delectable little Miss Maggie Mouse in the right place or the right way.

"I owe you a foot massage," he said, "for the one you gave me last night."

"Careful you don't put me to sleep!"

Oh, he had no intention of putting her to sleep. When she quit struggling, he lifted her foot to his mouth.

"Oh, don't," she whispered, entranced.

So, of course he did. He planted a lingering kiss on her instep.

She went very still and he reminded himself to take it slow. Even so, he ran a finger down the bottom of her foot from toe to heel and enjoyed the power of making her shiver.

"Are you sure you don't like to be tickled, Miss Maggie Mouse?"

"Positive," she said, but her cheeks were flushed and her eyes were heated as she yanked her foot away from him and stuffed it back in her boot.

"Race you," she said.

"That's what I was afraid of."

In moments they were back on the bikes, roaring up and down little hills, and through little hollows, around tight turns.

When he finally managed to wrest the lead from her, he did a bit of showing off. He took air, and lots of it.

He threw his legs free of the bike. He twisted the handlebars back and forth. He landed hard and running, and glanced back. She had stopped.

He went back to her.

She had taken her helmet off and was staring at him, not looking too impressed with his great show.

"Do you think that was wise?" she asked.

"What do you mean?"

"You're just out of the hospital. What are the consequences if you reinjure your back?" Her face had that pinched, pained look it had had when she'd seen his wrecked motorcycle in the workshop.

"I didn't take that much air," he said, but he could feel himself resenting her. One thing he did not like was being controlled. Everyone who had ever tried it had ended up being very sorry.

She must have read something in his face correctly, because without another word she put her helmet back on. But she didn't go out on the track again. She went back to the parking area.

"I think that's enough for me for one day," she said. "I'm tired. And my nose feels sunburned."

He tried to see if this was a continuation of the trying to control him, but she appeared utterly sincere. He looked at his watch and was surprised to see the day had dissolved.

He was sorry that it had. He did not want to say goodbye to the day, despite the small conflict that had cast a shadow on it.

"You want to barbecue steaks at my place tonight?" he asked.

"No."

He squinted at her. If she was going to try and punish him for doing what he did best—living his life as if he was tobogganing—it was over right now. Before it started.

He felt the sharp sting of regret at the thought.

But he was granted a reprieve.

"It's my turn," she said. "You can come to my place for dinner."

"You can cook, too?"

"What do you mean 'too'?"

"I meant as well as riding a motorbike. And looking gorgeous." And feeling wonderful to wake up beside.

"No, I wasn't planning on cooking," she admitted, looking pleased at the compliment. He knew not nearly enough men had told Maggie she was gorgeous.

"I mean I can cook simple things like cookies and cake out of a box. Things like turkey dinner are out."

"I'm disappointed," he teased. "I wanted you to rush home and whip up a turkey dinner in the July heat."

"I know something better. I know where the best takeout in Portland is."

"You're on," he said. He knew they should sort it out right now, that thing that had happened back there. It was his life and his back, and nobody was going to tell him what to do with either of those things. To ask him not to take risks would be like asking him not to breathe.

On the other hand, it felt as if it would spoil the moment. He was not the best communicator and he would probably manage to offend her. Then she might retract her dinner invitation.

And every bachelor wanted to know where to get the best takeout in town.

Nine

Dumb, dumb, dumb, Maggie thought, hurrying along the corridor of her building and inserting her key into the lock of her own apartment.

What had she been thinking asking Luke to come here? She stepped inside and looked around. She had always loved her apartment. It was a third-floor walk-up in an historical brownstone close enough to Children's Connection that most days Maggie could walk to work. Her space was charming, with its plaster detail and oak floors and stained glass in the upper frames of the French-pane windows.

But it was an absolute mess! A spurned and depressed woman had inhabited it for several days—a woman who was sure her love life was over.

And so there was laundry unfolded in a basket on the

sofa, two empty tubs of Double Chocolate Madness ice cream on the coffee table, wool socks on the floor. In July! She couldn't help it, whenever she was under stress her feet got cold. There were unread newspapers, and magazines open to pages of thin, alluring models dressed in the kind of scanty things Maggie would never be able to wear.

She glanced at her watch. So little time, and so much to do. Thank God she had not offered to cook for him.

She whipped the apartment into shape, tossing everything onto and underneath her bed, and firmly shut the door. Then, her arms folded over her chest, she tried to evaluate her apartment through his eyes.

"Frou-frou," she decided, too much lace and dried flowers. She thought the apartment said rather too much about her: woman alone and with no prospects.

Her bedroom was the worst—layers and layers of white eyelet linens, and pillows, even the duvet cover white and feminine and pure somehow. Thankfully, they wouldn't be using that room tonight. Oh no, her common sense had prevailed this morning at his place. As much as she had wanted to turn into his embrace in that bed this morning, her voice of reason had warned her, *Way too fast, Maggie*.

She had no idea where the voice of her reason had been the other two nights when she had thrown herself at him like an unprincipled hussy, but it had, thankfully, emerged this morning in time to save her in a most vulnerable moment.

Waking up beside him, surrounded by the aroma of his skin, and swept away by the amusement in his green eyes, she was not sure how she had prevented herself from throwing caution to the wind and herself right at him.

Perhaps on those two other occasions, in a parking lot, in the front seat of a very small car there were built-in safety features. It really could, after all, only go so far in those fairly public places.

That had not been the case this morning! They had had all the privacy and all the room in the world. She shivered thinking about it, and focused on getting her apartment shipshape, dusting, vacuuming, and hiding the worst of the frilly knickknacks.

Finally, having the apartment looking good, she went into the bathroom.

Her heart sank as she regarded herself in the full-length mirror behind the door. She had wasted all that time on making her home look so wonderful, when she looked like this?

Her hair was a wind-tangled mess, her nose was very sunburned, and she was still wearing the jeans and shirt Luke had loaned her.

He hadn't had a full-length mirror, and all day she had convinced herself—partly because of how Luke was reacting to her—that she must somehow look ravishing in his clothes.

Now she saw nothing could be further from the truth. She looked like an extra for "The Beverly Hillbillies," and not the long-legged one in the short-shorts and polka-dot crop tops, either!

To Maggie's critical eye, those two tubs of ice cream had moved directly from the buckets and glommed onto her hips. It was not a pretty sight.

She showered quickly, pulled her hair into a pony-tail, and then chose an outfit not for its allure but for its disguising power. She wore black pants—slimming—

and a white tailored shirt, the shirttails hiding the worst of the bulges.

Her vial of NoWait was on the counter by the sink, and she remembered that to underscore the hopelessness of her loveless existence she had stopped using it.

"Well, I need you now," she said. She picked it up and chanted, "A little rub on the skin, and in no time you're thin." Only she didn't have two weeks, so she applied all four days' worth of doses that she had missed, plus an additional day for good measure.

"Work," she muttered. She was busy trying to hide the worst of the damage to her sunburned nose when there was a knock on the door.

Luke arrived right on time. His nose was as sunburned as hers, only it looked good on him. His short-sleeved sports shirt and belted shorts showed off his lean, hard muscles.

He was a man who would never need NoWait, no matter how many tubs of ice cream or decadent desserts he devoured.

He had flowers! A beautiful summer bouquet, with a pink rose at the center surrounded by yellow and white daisies and a few carnations.

For some reason the scent of the flowers seemed extra heady to her. She leaned into the bouquet and buried her nose in it.

She peeked at Luke and felt as if her heart stopped beating. He had obviously just showered, too, and his dark hair was damp and wavy. She could smell the heady scent of cologne, and the skin on his freshly shaven jaw and chin looked somehow as if it needed to be touched.

Suddenly it was very plain to Maggie what the greatest risk of all was. And it hadn't been going to his place last night.

The biggest risk of her life would be to seduce this man!

She didn't even know where the thought had come from. It certainly had been nowhere to be found this morning when she had been in an ideal position to mount a plan for seduction.

Oh who was she kidding? He called her Miss Maggie Mouse. She was no seductress and they both knew it. In fact, she was so exciting, she reminded herself a trifle peevishly, that she had put him right to sleep last night.

Still, she leaned toward him to thank him for the flowers. The clean lines of his cheeks and jaw still beckoned to her. It was going to be a quick peck on that fresh-shaven cheek, but somehow she missed his cheek and her lips touched his lips.

A glorious feeling swept over her, warm and liquid and all-encompassing. It was as if, in her belly, a few warm embers from a fire gone nearly dead still existed. That kiss breathed on them, made them flare and sputter to life, like a dragon awakening.

She stepped back from him, could feel the dragon's breath heating her cheeks to smoldering.

"I'll just put these in water," she said, ducking away from him. "Come in."

He followed her through to the kitchen. "I like your place, Maggie, all warm and cozy, just like you."

If only he knew! Right now the last thing she was feeling was warm and cozy. She was feeling white-hot and ready to go.

She had a computer center set up in a little nook in

the kitchen, a Scrabble board set up on it, next to the computer. It was a testament to the loneliness of her life for the past few years that she had come to take such enjoyment from her ongoing Internet matches. She actually kept the board set up, kept track of her moves and the opponent's, rehearsed different moves out here before she submitted them.

"Scrabble," he said. "You'll have to show me how to play sometime."

This was said with such an utter lack of sincerity that he might as well have said she was dull and unexciting, the eccentric spinster her apartment heralded.

She turned and eyed him narrowly. Frankly she had had enough of Luke August finding her amusing and interesting but infinitely resistible.

She dropped the flowers in the sink but made no move to find a vase for them. She moved across the floor to him with deliberation. The taste of his lips was still on her own lips, heady and as inhibition-killing as wine.

Her intent must have been in her face because he actually backed up a step. "I don't think this is how you play Scrabble," he said.

She stopped right in front of him, felt this strange and intoxicating boldness filling her.

"First, you pick a letter," she said, then leaned around him and pulled a tile from the box. "Oh my, it's a *K*."

"That's a good thing?" he asked warily.

She took his shirt, wrapped it around her fist and drew him close to her.

"I believe it's the first letter in *kiss*," she said. And then she did. She kissed him. She kissed him with a complete lack of reservation. She kissed him, releasing all that heat that had been building up inside her, not just since she had met him, but since she had been left by Darnel. Maggie had tried so hard to extinguish all about herself that was passionate and needy and vulnerable.

She saw now she had not succeeded. She had buried, not extinguished. And everything, years of pent-up frustration and desire, had just been waiting for her to lift the lid off that buried treasure of her desire.

She kissed him recklessly, until she was dizzy from it. She released his shirt and swayed back.

"I think I might like Scrabble," he said, dazed.

She reached back into the box and picked out another letter.

"Oh," she said, "you got an *I*."

"The second letter in kiss?" he guessed.

"You catch on very quickly."

He gathered her in his arms, and his lips claimed hers, welcoming, demanding, teasing, taking. The first kiss had revealed a glitter, a hint of the treasure in her buried subconscious chest. Now the lid blew off, revealing the full intensity of what was in her, abundant, rich and beautiful.

Her apartment faded from her awareness. And so did the flowers in the sink, and the Scrabble board. She felt as though she had eaten only bread her entire life and suddenly discovered something exotic and faintly sinful, like lobster.

His lips tasted of sin and sensuality and raindrops and heaven.

"Your turn," he said, barely lifting his lips off hers. He reached behind them and held out the game lid, full of letters, for her.

Trembling faintly, she reached back into the box.

"That better be an *S*," he told her, setting the lid back down, his forehead leaning against hers, his chest rising and falling in ragged gasps.

She glanced at the letter. "It's not. It's an *F*."

He reeled back from her. "Lordie, I'm scared to ask."

"By itself it means nothing," she said and drew another letter. "Hmm, an *R*."

"Does it mean anything yet?"

She shook her head and drew another letter. "Oh, it's an *E*." She smacked herself playfully on the forehead. "I should have got it sooner."

"What?" he asked hoarsely.

"It's *French,* of course,"

"I thought you couldn't use proper nouns," he said, but his lips were already making a trail down her face, touching her forehead, her eyelids, the tip of her nose, until they came to her lips.

"I thought you didn't know anything about this game," she pouted.

"I'm probably mistaken." His lips found hers, and his tongue flicked the plumpness of her bottom lip.

"You can challenge *French* if you want to," she murmured.

"What happens if I challenge?"

"No *French.*"

"No challenge from me." And then his tongue darted in her mouth, ran along the rough bottom edges of her front teeth, plundered her tongue.

The intimacy of the kiss was the most exquisite of tortures, delightful, painful, tormenting, teasing. The kiss was fanning that fire within her, the heat building, begging to be extinguished.

Only one thing could release this tender agony within her.

"Is that how you'd interpret *French?*" he asked her, his lips on her ear, his breath hot and sweet and sending tingles up and down her spine.

"Exactly."

"My turn," he gasped against her ear. He pulled a tile. "It's a *B.*"

"And?"

"It stands for *button*. This one right here." And with his index finger he flicked open the top button of her blouse. He traced the line of her throat to just beneath where that button was, the soft swell at the top of her breast.

"How many *B*s in that box?" he asked.

"Two."

"That isn't going to be enough."

"You could substitute an *F,* for, um, *fastener.*"

"How many of those?"

"Two."

"And we've already used one," he reminded her.

"You may be out of luck, then."

He swore softly, and she put back her head and laughed throatily, which earned her a kiss right in the hollow of her throat, followed by a white-hot flick of the tip of his tongue.

"Then again," he said, "I could be creative. As in the letter *U* for *undo.*"

"Exactly," she told him. "There are four of those."

"*E* for *earlobes.*" He kissed her there. "*M* for *mouth.* Oh yeah, and *X* for *X-rated.* I really like Scrabble. Who would have imagined?"

"Not me," she admitted. In fact, even ten minutes ago

she could not have imagined that her life was going to move in this direction.

He let go of her long enough to look at the board. "Look at all the scores on here," he mused, and began counting the colored squares. "Good grief, you can score about a hundred times playing this game."

"Sometimes you can double and triple score," she told him.

He sighed blissfully. "I missed the point of this game entirely. I did play once in eighth grade. I made a mistake. I thought it was boring."

"Actually, I'm a little bored with Scrabble now," she said.

"We were just getting started," he protested.

"Want to switch to Trouble?"

"Only if it's half as good as it sounds."

"Oh, believe me, it is." The new Maggie, bold and beautiful, took his hand and led him to the closed door of her bedroom.

"I'm giving you the Monopoly," she said.

"You won't be Sorry."

They cracked up laughing, and somehow that was as she had hoped it would be, light and laughter-filled, so that he would never have a clue how rarely she played this particular game in her life.

But even as she led him through the door, her laundry piled on the bed tried to remind her she might be in Jeopardy.

That she was being impulsive and that she might indeed be Sorry after all.

But she didn't want to worry about after. For once in her life, Maggie Sullivan was determined to embrace the here and now, to take what was being offered to her without questioning and analyzing and spoiling everything.

She tossed the laundry on the floor and fell backward on the bed, holding out her arms to him.

"Whoo boy," he said and toppled on top of her, holding some of his weight back with braced arms.

She traced the line of a taut arm muscle and smiled. "Has anyone ever told you you're a Masterpiece?"

"I didn't have a Clue."

Their laughter mingled until he lowered himself and his chest was pressed hard against the curve of her breast. He took her lips again. "Speaking of masterpieces..." His hands found the elastic that bound her hair. "You look better like this."

He gently unraveled the fastener and her hair cascaded down over her shoulders. He buried his face in it, breathing deeply.

"I think you mentioned something about Trouble," he reminded her huskily.

"Time to use up that other *B*," she said.

And he did, flicking open the next button of her blouse and finding the delicate skin with his tongue.

Soon the buttons were all undone and her blouse was open.

He gazed at the red bra, all lace and film, that she had bought to go with her red dress, and drew in his breath sharply.

"It's almost too pretty to take off," he whispered. He touched the lace with his thumb, rubbed it slowly and erotically across the peak of her breast.

The fabric barrier between his hands and her skin was sharply, beautifully sensual.

She tried to twine her hands around his neck, to pull him to her, to feel his shirt on the bareness of her skin, but he smiled and pinned her arms on either side of her head.

"Not so fast, Maggie. This is a game of brains. I have to think very carefully about my next move."

Still using both his arms to pin hers, he lowered his head to where his thumb had played seconds before.

He breathed, deliberately, slowly, the heat of his breath penetrating the silk of the undergarment. She wriggled against him.

"Uh-uh, my turn isn't finished," he said. He ran his tongue between her collarbones, let it dance in the hollow of her throat, moved lower, his tongue blazing a trail of fire between her breasts.

Then he flicked with his tongue underneath the boundary of that brassiere. Slowly, taking his time, he explored those boundaries, checking out his limits with fiendish delight, raising his eyebrows wickedly at her gasps and sighs. Then, when he could go no further, he reached behind her and loosed the clasp of her bra, opening new and unexplored territory.

"Risk," he explained to her. "I've just taken over new territory." He lifted the bra, tugged and it fell away. "To the conqueror go the spoils."

He was very silent for a moment, and very still. His eyes drank in what he had revealed, and then raised to her face.

"You are the most beautiful woman I have ever seen," he whispered hoarsely, and then the talking was done.

He lowered his head once more, let go of her wrists.

She put her arms around his neck, pulling him closer as his tongue did its dance of fire.

"How many turns do you get?" she finally panted.

"I'm a poor sport," he admitted, his voice gravelly.

"It's my turn," she insisted, and he stopped what he was doing and knelt above her, his knees forming a V around her rib cage.

She reached up and slid her hands underneath his shirt, tugged at the hem of it. He ducked his head, and the shirt came off. She cast it away and stared.

She looked her fill of him—the cut of muscle and bone, the hard beauty of a man. And then she touched him. His skin was warm, the contrast of its softness over the uncompromising steel of his muscle glorious to touch.

He leaned back over her, and his mouth took hers.

There was more urgency to the way he removed her slacks, and she his shorts.

They were naked together on top of all that white eyelet, the sultry July breeze cooling skin that was becoming sweat-beaded.

He touched her and kissed her in ways and places that made her feel as if all her life she had only pretended to be a woman.

Now, finally, she was finding out what it truly was to want with insane hunger, to feel with feeling so deep and hard it crossed pleasure with pain, to desire joining her body with his in so primal a way it was as if nothing of Maggie existed except that single ragged, raging want.

Everything she had been up until that moment—a social worker, a daughter, a college graduate, a spurned woman—each of those things that she had used to define herself was erased.

Her history was obliterated by the look in green eyes

gone dark as night. Swept away by hands that stroked and stoked, feathered and fondled, commanded and cradled.

"Maggie," he said hoarsely, poised above her, a fine tremble in his voice and in the corded muscles of his arms, "are you sure?"

She was sure.

And she answered him by opening to him like a moon-flower to moonlight, by pressing herself so close to him the lines between them blurred, and they became one.

She answered him by taking his lips with hers with a wanting so primal it shook them both.

He accepted her answer and entered her with the surging power of the incoming tide. She rose to meet him, rock to rogue wave. And the union was just as spectacular, cataclysmic.

She was drowning in sensation, rising toward fulfillment, drowning again.

And then she was there—at that place where body meets soul and mind meets spirit, and all things melt into one.

She was there with him, crying out, sobbing her joy and rapture, clinging to him, wanting the waves of pleasure to roll on forever.

She looked at him, deeply, and let go. Sensation such as this could never be captured. Could never go on forever.

But she had seen what she needed to see in his eyes.

And if it was not forever, then there was no such thing.

Luke had one arm under his neck, the other around Maggie. She was fast asleep and he watched her curtains jig with the wind, felt the touch of the breeze on the salt of his skin.

He had lived a life where he chased the unexpected. He loved nothing more than surprises, the unpredictable.

But nothing in his experience had prepared him for the utter surprise of Maggie.

The woman was red-hot.

Under that cool, composed Miss Maggie Mouse exterior was the woman every man dreamed about and fantasized about. She was playful, joyous, giving, curious, bold.

Add to that what she was outside the bedroom: intelligent, compassionate, thoughtful, funny.

Miss Maggie Mouse was the perfect woman.

And he was pretty darn sure if he wasn't in love with her already he was going to be before he knew it.

Love. The last thing he'd been looking for in his life.

Truth be told, he wasn't sure if he cared for what love did to people, making them grasp at each other, try for control, try to own.

But maybe his mother had been right at lunch the other day. Maybe Luke just had all the wrong ideas because he had been raised in a home where security had masqueraded as love, and where love had been held out with a price tag.

If you behaved in such and such a way, then you earned love.

It had never been given freely to him. Not in his entire life, beginning with his mother, but not ending there.

There had been dozens of relationships that had looked promising, and that had always ended much the same way.

Women wanted to change him. The qualities they first found exciting—his love of adventure, his hair-straight-back approach to life—ended up scaring them, threatening their security.

He remembered Maggie that day at the dirt bike track.

Worried about his back. Or worried about how his hurt back might affect her?

He got up restlessly. Her room was a mess. There was clean laundry in a flattened heap on the floor. They had made love on top of that once. There were take-out food boxes from Flying Pie Pizzeria. The Scrabble board, moved in from the kitchen sometime during the night, was turned over and there were tiles everywhere.

All in all he couldn't remember having a more satisfying night.

He wished it was not ending with these questions and doubts.

He watched the sun peep up over the horizon, then turned and found his clothing somewhere in the heap.

He'd go get breakfast somewhere and bring it back for her.

And then?

Then he was putting her to the test, before he got into this thing so deep there would be no pulling back.

An hour later, they had both called into work to say they would be late.

She nibbled on a croissant and sipped the frothy flavored coffee he had brought her.

Her eyes were hungry and full of promise, and she looked sexy sitting at the table in his shirt and nothing else.

"Want to go back to bed?" she asked.

"Maggie, you are showing every sign of being a very bad girl."

"I know," she said so happily that he had to laugh.

Get it over with, he thought miserably. He took out the piece of paper he had retrieved from the saddlebag of his Harley on the way back from the corner bakery.

"I'm entering this," he said casually.

She looked at the paper with curiosity.

Across the top in huge bold red letters, it said: Death Defiers: The Most Challenging Moto-Cross Race in Oregon.

Leo held it every year. It was an excellent off-road motorcycle course. Each year Leo added new obstacles and new challenges.

She read the entry form through thoroughly. She did not miss anything. He knew the exact moment she read the disclaimer saying that racing dirt bikes was an extremely dangerous sport, that death and serious injury could occur.

He watched the blood drain from her face. He hated himself.

But that was who he was. A death defier. An adrenaline junkie. He could not change that for her.

"Luke, this race is a week away. You are just barely out of the hospital."

Here it came, then.

"I know," he said breezily. He took a big bite out of his croissant.

"I don't think you should do this," she said. She looked at the paper again, shoved it across the table to him and wouldn't look at him.

"Because I'm just out of the hospital?"

She nodded.

"So, when would you think it was okay for me to enter a race like this?"

Her eyes met his, and he saw the answer in them. *Never.* It was never going to be okay with her.

"Maggie," he said softly, "it's part of who I am. I am entering this race."

"I have to get ready for work," she said dully.

She didn't even finish her croissant. She went to her bedroom and shut the door, a certain finality in the click.

He wasn't sure what to make of that. She was supposed to scream and yell and try to get her way. She was supposed to want to talk about it. Women always wanted to talk.

He went to the bedroom door. "Hey, can I have my shirt?"

The door opened a crack and the shirt hit him with some force, midchest.

"Do you want to talk about this?"

"No." The door closed.

"I'll call you later."

He pulled on his shirt. She was sure to change her mind. She'd have gathered all her arguments and be ready to talk then.

But she didn't answer through the closed door. He glared at it. He wondered if he was really willing to risk the joy he'd found in her arms for the temporary thrill of revving engines and sky-rocketing adrenaline.

The stubborn male in him answered immediately, yes. He stomped down the hallway and through her kitchen. He didn't pick up the entry form from where it lay on her table. He left it there to remind her, when all the fun and games were over, he was still who he was. He wasn't changing. He wasn't sure he could, even if he wanted to.

Which he didn't.

Ten

W hen Maggie emerged from her bedroom, Luke was gone. He'd left his entry form for the race on her kitchen table, but she knew it was too much to hope that it might mean he was going to reconsider.

She was sorry he was gone. He really should see her like this. Maggie had dressed very primly in an outfit nearly as inspiring as her porridge-colored one, this one as gray as a Portland winter day.

The truth was she wanted to disguise that thing she had released in herself last night. The tigress had to be put back in her cage.

But just thinking of last night, she felt that weakness in her belly that made her wonder just how much control she had. Once you had let a force like that out, something so powerful and untamed, could you really lock it back up?

Or did you become one of those people who kissed shamelessly and wantonly on public staircases and in little booths at the back of pubs?

She understood that kind of behavior better than she ever had before, and her understanding perturbed her.

In defiance of it, she crossed her kitchen, picked Luke's entry form off her table and crumpled it. She tossed it in the garbage. "Death defiers be damned," she said.

She had always known the sad truth. Even before Darnel, she had been the girl most likely to take the safe way, least likely to have any kind of adventure. She was the one who should live in Boring! Maggie liked predictability, stability, routine, safety.

After Darnel, that longing for the world to be a safe place and a predictable place had intensified.

A woman who harbored a passionate longing to be safe could not be with a man like Luke, a man who flirted with danger and danced with death. She could not, rationally, be with a man who took such a cavalier attitude toward his own life.

If Darnel's leaving had hurt her deeply, left her feeling shattered, what was it going to do to her if something happened to Luke? The hard truth of the matter was she had not had nearly the intensity of feeling for Darnel that she had for Luke. And she'd only known Luke such a short time. Her feelings for him would grow stronger, if she allowed them to, and the pain he was capable of causing her could worsen.

If Luke died, even now, after this short acquaintance, Maggie was not sure she could survive the pain of it.

She was not even sure she could survive the pain

of his desire to pursue activities that were billed as death-defying.

Death would only be defied so many times before it claimed its prize.

Luke had been in the hospital seven times in five years. If he was a cat that would mean he was using up his lives rather rapidly.

Maggie did not really want to go to work this morning. In the days after Darnel had abandoned her she had taken to her bed and cried until she had no tears left.

It had not, she reminded herself firmly, solved anything.

What had saved her had been her return to work. There was always so much to do there; she always had a feeling of impacting lives in such a positive way. And so she was going there now. To lose herself, not even to think she was being abandoned again, in quite a different way.

She went to the office. Maggie worked and worked and worked. She worked until long after everyone else had gone home. It was not nearly the balm she had hoped it would be. At odd moments she became aware she was staring off into space, reliving the night before, wanting that feeling again so badly. It felt as if the tears were bottling up inside her, too much rainwater adding to an already full dam. Her head ached from it, and it felt as though it would only be a matter of time until all that feeling burst out of her, overflowing the walls of that dam. Still, she worked harder trying to hold off the catastrophe of feeling too deeply.

Finally, she put away her papers, exhausted and numb. She came out of her office building to find Kristen just coming up the front walkway. They met on the steps.

"I was just coming to find you. Did you forget? It's our last Bold and Beautiful seminar tonight."

"I didn't forget. I'm not going." Maggie's voice sounded wooden and so far away, disconnected from her person.

Kristen looked at her closely. "Oh, God," she said with pleasure. "You are so in love."

"I am not." If this was love—all this angst and pain and doubt, and wanting things you couldn't have or that came at too great a price tag—then Kristen could have it!

"You are. Up one day, down the next. Up, down. Up, down. It's the roller-coaster ride, and, Maggie, it's the greatest ride on the face of the earth."

The tears pushed against the back of her eyes. "Nonsense," she said with stiff control. She was saved from Kristen's all-seeing scrutiny by the throaty sound of a large motorcycle. She and Kristen both turned to look, but Maggie was willing to bet only one of their hearts had begun racing a mile a minute.

Luke was pulling up to the curb on the Harley. He looked so extraordinarily handsome in his black leather, big, self-assured, faintly dangerous. Maggie reminded herself that it was that dangerous part that was the whole problem. Damnably attractive, but problematic.

He pulled off the helmet, tucked it under his arm, shook free his hair, which was adorably spiked from being under the helmet. He hooked a leg over the saddle.

Maggie felt that old swooning feeling coming over her and stiffened her spine. She had to be strong.

"Hey, pretty lady, I've been calling your place. I thought I could talk you into a game of Scrabble. Or a moonlight ride on my motorbike."

Maggie shot a glance at Kristen. Her mouth was hanging open. She glanced at Maggie and mouthed her astonishment. *This is him?*

It reminded Maggie sharply that no one, not even her best friend, expected Maggie Mouse to be invited on moonlight motorbike rides with a man like this. It reminded Maggie she had bitten off way more than she could handle with Luke August.

"Isn't that the bike from the movie *Terminator?*" Kristen asked, going to the curb and running a polished fingernail over the Harley symbol on the gas tank.

Maggie watched as her friend tossed her head of red corkscrew curls and grinned her irresistible grin.

Why hadn't she thought of that before? Her best friend and Luke would make an astounding match. They were both beautiful people.

But the very thought of surrendering Luke to anyone was very upsetting. Didn't she have an ounce of gumption, an ounce of fight?

Confusion overwhelmed her. Why would she fight for a man who had a death wish? With whom she had made the firm decision she was not pursuing a relationship?

How could a decision like that be firm in the face of this? He was so close! She wanted to run down the steps and throw herself into his arms, kiss him all over, ride away into the moonlight with him forever.

Except that was the problem. Luke August was constantly challenging the concept of forever. He would make Maggie into a mess of jangled nerves. She'd spend her life wringing her hands and developing those worry wrinkles on her forehead.

Kristen was extending her hand to him. Maggie noticed he took Kristen's hand briefly and then sent Maggie a pleading "rescue me" look. What kind of man preferred Maggie to Kristen?

The kind of man, she reminded herself, who took his life in his hands as a matter of course. Who had no consideration for the feelings and sensitivities of others.

But superimposing themselves over that very rational conclusion were memories of last night, flooding her with heat and wanting. She had to get rid of him, and quickly!

"I can't go for a motorbike ride," Maggie said stiffly. "It's my last Bold and Beautiful seminar tonight."

She noticed that she did not close the door completely. She did not tell him to ride off into the sunset without her for good.

For good, now that the concept had entered her mind, seemed like an unbearably long time without him.

He kicked the stand under the bike, got off it and strode toward her. Kristen was barely more than a speck to him as he brushed by her.

"You don't need any lessons in being bold or beautiful," he told her gruffly. "You have both those qualities in abundance."

"Apparently not enough to convince you to stop taking ridiculous and unnecessary risks with your life!"

"Maggie, this thing between us is not about you telling me how to live."

Put like that, she almost thought maybe he was right and she was wrong. But then that was what a man like this did—knocked all your compass headings off kilter so you didn't know anymore what was up, what was down, what was right, what was wrong.

"I'm going to the seminar," she said. Maybe she would hear something that would help her get her bearings, sort through this chaos of feeling and confusion within her.

"I think we need to talk," he growled. Unless she was mistaken, he was giving her an order! Oh! How dare he be so sexy and masterful? It made it all the harder to stand her ground.

But stand her ground she did. "I can't tonight."

Again, she noticed she had not closed the door completely, and it wasn't totally because she did not want to humiliate him in front of her friend.

Humiliate him.

Miss Maggie Mouse humiliating him. It seemed so absurd she thought for a moment she might laugh, but then realized it was nerves.

Having him stand so close to her, his scent masked only faintly by leather and motorcycle smells, Maggie was awash again in memories of last night, the primal and erotic beauty of the time they had spent together. How could a woman think straight under these circumstances?

"What time are you done with your class?" he asked. He reached out and touched her hair. The gesture was tender and possessive, as if he was saying to all the world, and the avidly watching Kristen, *This is my woman.* Maggie felt a shiver down to the bottom of her socks.

"Not until late," she said. "Too late."

Disappointment clouded the green of his eyes. His hand dropped back to his side.

Kristen had materialized beside her and gave her a sharp dig in the ribs with her elbow. "Don't be an idiot," she hissed and pushed Maggie none too gently toward Luke.

But Maggie dug in her heels and folded her arms over her chest.

Luke eyed her shrewdly, put his helmet back on, gave her a slow salute, and then sauntered over to his bike, all loose-limbed grace, and swung a long leg over it. The engine started with a throaty, powerful purr, and then he was pulling smoothly into traffic, leaving her.

For good?

Kristen whirled on her. "Have you lost your ever-loving mind?"

Maggie had, but that was last night.

"No," she said, but she was not so sure. She knew she was losing everything, not just her mind, but everything that mattered somehow.

"Was he serious? Scrabble?"

"Possibly."

"Maggie, he's a perfect ten! He's like a movie star, only ten times better. He's rugged and real and about the sexiest thing I've ever seen. He wanted you to go with him!"

"Yes," Maggie said.

"Did you see the look on his face when he touched your hair?"

"Yes," she whispered.

"That man is crazy in love with you."

Crazy in love with her. Maggie digested that. Could it possibly be true? She had to remind herself, firmly, that he was not so crazy in love with her that he wanted to live instead of die.

"Oh, I could just strangle you sometimes," Kristen said.

"Well, today would be a real good day if you plan to do it."

"Oh, come on," Kristen said. "Let's see if Dr. Richie can talk some sense into you."

"Actually, I have come to my senses."

Kristen snorted. "I don't think so," she said dramatically.

She paused in the door of the class, and her annoyance at Maggie evaporated. "Maggie," she said excitedly, "look over there."

Maggie looked at a beautiful woman standing off to the side as the rest of the class took their seats. The woman was tall and willowy and masses of red curly hair haloed her extraordinarily stunning face. It was a face that would not be forgotten, once seen, and Maggie had a vague sense of knowing who the woman was.

"It's the film star," Kristen whispered, awed. "Cynthia Reynolds."

"It is not," Maggie said, but she could see Kristen was convinced. She felt a moment's gratitude that at least it was taking her friend's mind off their encounter with Luke.

"I'm going to ask her," Kristen said.

Maggie looked back at the woman. Despite her great beauty, or maybe because of it, she looked like she might enjoy her privacy, but Kristen was generally not sensitive to such subtle vibes. There was, in fact, no talking to Kristen once she got that look in her eye. Thank goodness that look was now being directed at someone else!

Kristen came back a few minutes later, breathless. "It *is* her!"

Maggie tried to look suitably awed. The truth was Brad Pitt could run through the room naked right now and she could barely make herself care about it.

Glumly, she took her seat while Kristen looked around for something to have the film star autograph.

"Not a piece of paper," she muttered. "Something that could become a collectible." She leaned forward to the woman in front of her. "Do you think I could buy your scarf from you? That's Cynthia Reynolds over there, and I'd like her to sign something for me."

The woman looked over where Kristen was pointing, and leaped up. Moments later, Kristen was watching with narrowed eyes as the woman had Cynthia sign her scarf.

"Of all the nerve," Kristen muttered.

Dr. Richie came in. He didn't make any fuss over the new member of the class, though he was obviously very aware she was there.

Maggie wondered if this was her fate now: would every man be compared to Luke and found wanting? Because she found herself looking at Dr. Richie and seeing things she had not seen before. She was very aware that he was subtly preening for Cynthia Reynolds and smiling nervously, like a person with stage fright. Maggie was willing to bet the star had asked him not to introduce her or draw attention to her. She was also willing to bet he desperately wanted to do just that.

Kristen continued to focus on the film star, and Maggie continued to focus on the chaos her life had become.

At the break she intended to sneak out and not come back. How could anyone here shed any light on the mess her life had become? It was back to her couch, and Double Chocolate Madness.

"Well," Dr. Richie said, beaming, "it's our last night together. I hope everyone has discovered the boldness and the beauty of the new you."

Maggie thought she had discovered the boldness of the new her, all right. She just wasn't at all sure it was a good thing.

Her mind wandered. She thought of Luke. She thought of him telling her, with such tender sincerity, that she already had those qualities in abundance. She thought of their night together. She thought of the look of boyish delight on his face as he had pulled up on the motorcycle outside just now. She thought of Kristen saying, "That man is crazy in love with you."

Since it was the final class, Dr. Richie reminded everyone that his new series of seminars, called Losing Weight Through Visualization would be starting shortly.

This seemed to be directed personally at the film star.

Maggie glanced over at her and didn't think the gorgeous Miss Reynolds looked as if she needed to lose any weight. She was curvy, yes, but in that way of a woman maturing, coming fully into herself.

"Because it is our last night," Dr. Richie said, "perhaps some of you could share with me the changes this seminar has made in your lives."

The testimonials were enthusiastic and numerous. Maggie was not sure she could bear listening to one more person say how happy they were, how the B&B seminars and NoWait seemed to have changed their lives. They felt more energetic. More alive. More passionate.

Well, she could add an "and how" to that last one. Actually, she had to admit she could say yes to all those things.

"I have a final challenge for you," Dr. Richie said, "before we say adieu."

He paused, steepled his fingers thoughtfully under

his nose, and when he spoke again, his voice had changed. It seemed as if it was coming from a place deep, deep within himself.

"Sometimes," he said quietly, "we have a stranglehold on life. We exhaust ourselves and milk the joy from life by trying to be in control of everything, including other people. The truth is that we only have control over one small thing in this world. And that one small thing is ourselves."

Maggie found herself listening, truly listening, for the first time tonight.

Dr. Richie went on. "We need to give up our need to control everything. We need to surrender to the process of life, to trust it."

Maggie stared at him. It seemed as though he was speaking directly to her. And suddenly he did turn and look right at her.

She was aware, from the sympathetic look on his face, that she might not be looking her best.

But nothing about the way Luke had looked at her just a few minutes ago had made her feel the way Dr. Richie's gaze was making her feel—as if she should rush off and change clothes, brush her hair, apply a dab of lipstick.

"There is one thing you are holding on to," Dr. Richie said, his voice sage, his eyes locked on hers, despite the presence of the movie star in their midst. "Let it go."

Let it go. She stared back at him. She felt as if he had seen right into her heart, exposed her deepest fears and insecurities, and told her exactly what she needed to do.

Let it go.

She scrambled up from her chair, nearly knocking it over.

Kristen sighed and rolled her eyes. "I hope you have come to your senses."

"I think I have," Maggie said.

"Good. Go call that man and ride in the moonlight. I don't know about the Scrabble part, though."

Maggie smiled. "That was the best part."

"So, are you going to call him?"

"Excuse me," a woman beside them said. "Must you two girls be so disruptive?"

They ignored the question. "No," Maggie said to her friend, "I am not going to call him."

Kristen glared at her. "Then you're crazy."

Maggie actually laughed. "I think I am," she said. *Crazy in love.* She raced out the doors of the Healthy Living Clinic and practically ran all the way home.

She arrived breathless, picked up the phone the minute she got in the door, and crossed her fingers. But she did not call Luke August.

No, she called Skookum Leo's, and nearly cried with relief when he was there and answered his phone.

Calmly, firmly, she made her request.

And then she called her office and left a message on her secretary's voice mail. No doubt the woman would be surprised in the morning.

"She's not here for the rest of the week, sir."

Luke couldn't believe his ears. Maggie was not answering her phone at home, and now she was not at work, either?

"Well, where is she?" he growled.

"Sir, even if I had that information I would not give it to every stranger who called in," he was told snippily.

He was so crazy in love he actually appreciated that her secretary was so protective of her.

Crazy in love. This couldn't be happening to him, Luke August, but it was and there was no hiding it. It was in his face every single time he failed to make contact with her. For a little Maggie Mouse, she was showing amazing stubbornness. She wouldn't return his calls and was avoiding him with great success.

Well, he'd played this game before. Of course, before he had always been on the other end of the avoiding game.

So, he was being brushed off. He was just going to have to accept that. He should be grateful that he was thirty-four years old and had never had this horrible experience before—the experience of being on this side of unrequited love.

He was miserable. He couldn't eat. He couldn't sleep. He yelled at Brian. He called his mother. He bought a puppy that he called Stinkbomb, Too. It promptly lived up to its name by depositing a steaming brown pile on the new carpet in his house.

The dog was supposed to replace Maggie. It was supposed to take his mind off her. It was supposed to meet his need for love and attention.

And really, the poor creature was no better at any of those things than Amber had been.

Luke was like a lovesick boy and it was embarrassing. He actually considered canceling the race, phoning and telling her.

But he stopped short of that. It felt all wrong. Agreeing not to ride in the race would be more than surrender, it would be utter defeat. He would be giving a part of himself away. And if he did that now, this early in the relationship, what would be left of him by the time little Miss Maggie was through with him?

"Remember Samson," he told himself and the dog. "Crazy in love with Delilah. Gave his power to her. That was the message. It's not real love if it takes your power."

Stinkbomb, Too cocked his head this way and that, and looked at Luke with rapt adoration.

"She appears to be through with me now," Luke told the dog after he'd tried her number for about the hundredth time and gotten no answer. The dog whined sympathetically.

"So, I go on with my life. I enter that race on Saturday. And I bet I win, too."

They were the sentiments of a man who had nothing to lose, who could pull out what few stops he had ever exercised in his life.

But despite his resolve to put Maggie out of his mind, he did not succeed. In unguarded moments that wild night with her would enter his mind and fill him with the most intense longing. She was in his dreams. He caught himself having imaginary conversations with her.

He was crazy in love, and the humiliating fact was that everyone knew. Brian knew. His mother knew. Even Rhonda down at Morgan's knew.

It was as if he had a big flashing sign on his head that said "Luke August has fallen and fallen hard."

"You got it bad," Brian told him, not without satisfaction.

"I don't," Luke snapped. "It's over."

Brian regarded him with a faintly sympathetic smirk.

"No, it ain't, boss. This is just the beginning. It's like a roller-coaster ride. Up, down. Up again. Hang in there."

It was a sad state of affairs when a guy like Brian was giving advice to the lovelorn.

His mother guessed when he told her he'd bought a dog. How did women do that—make these leaps that defied logic, and that were almost always right?

"Hey, Ma," he said wearily, "do you want to come watch me race my motorcycle this weekend?"

He expected the lecture. Maybe he actually even craved it. He could feel much better about the mess his relationship with Maggie was in, if all women were the same. If they all nagged and worried unnecessarily, and manipulated to get their own way. His mother's reaction to the invite could serve as a great reminder that he was lucky Maggie was not returning his calls. He was lucky he was still free. Lucky to still be his own man, with no one and nothing to answer to.

But his mother did not get with the program. "Why, I'd be delighted!" she shocked him by answering.

He went to Morgan's once, hoping he might see Maggie there, even though he knew the possibility was beyond remote. Rhonda asked where she was, and then said, out of the blue, "You got a thing for her, Luke?"

"No!" he growled.

But Rhonda had smiled that annoying little female smile that said she knew something that he didn't know.

Race day arrived, and Luke was frazzled, but glad to be here. There was nothing that required intensity of focus so much as climbing dirt hills and sliding around tight corners on a powerful bike. The concentration required to ride a race like this would be a total reprieve from his own Maggie-induced insanity.

He unloaded his bike from the trailer behind his truck. He began to don gear, checked over the bike.

"Hey, Luke!"

He turned in surprise. Billy was behind him in his wheelchair. Pushing it was Nurse Nightmare, looking very out of place in high-waisted jeans and a primly buttoned blouse.

"Hey, buddy." He went over and high-fived the boy. He could feel his heart beating fast. "How'd you hear about this?"

"Maggie," Billy said.

Maggie. It confirmed what Luke had thought as soon as he had seen the boy. She was the only reason Billy would be here.

She had forgiven him. Luke just knew it. She had forgiven him and come to watch, and brought Billy with her.

She had accepted who he was. She'd been mulling it over for the better part of a week and reached her conclusion. Now she was here to cheer him on!

The relief he felt was immense. Relief mingled with amazement and wonder and gratitude. Did she love him after all? Was there hope? His life seemed to be going from black and white to full blazing color at the very thought. He had not realized the full extent of his agony until this happened, a promise it was going to be over soon, a hope that it might all turn out all right after all.

Brian had been right. It was a roller-coaster ride. His mother had been right. Rhonda had been right. Luke needed her. Wanted her. He looked around, his heart on fire for wanting to see her.

But he didn't see her, and doubt began to cloud the momentary euphoria he had felt. If Maggie had brought Billy, why was Nurse Wagner here with him?

"Uh, where is Maggie?" Luke asked.

Billy shrugged. "She said I'd see her here." He turned his attention toward a commotion going on down by the announcer's booth.

Luke looked over, too. A cluster of riders—most of the men he recognized as seasoned racers on this circuit— had formed a circle around a rider he didn't recognize.

No wonder the fuss. She was fully outfitted for a motocross race, filling out her leather pretty nicely. She was wearing the red number that designated riders in the novice division.

The guys were high-fiving her as if they were her pit crew. Nigel Henderson was probably the best racer on this circuit, and Luke couldn't ever remember him making a fuss over a novice, not even a female one. Leo himself pushed to the center of the circle of boisterous bikers and wrapped a brawny arm around her shoulder.

"Is she ready or what?" he bellowed.

The guys gathered around her responded with the enthusiasm of Romans waiting for the gladiators to enter the Colosseum.

The female rider ducked her head, tugged at the chin-strap of her helmet, and then pulled it off, setting free a cascade of hair.

Luke felt his heart stop when the rider shook her head and that rich blond hair spilled out from under the helmet and over the padding on her shoulders.

"Oh, no," he whispered.

By chance, she turned and looked toward him. The

last time he had seen her that flushed with happiness she had been naked in his arms.

There was no doubt about it. It was his one true love. It was Maggie.

Eleven

Luke crossed the distance between him and Maggie in about three long strides. He ignored the protests of the fan club clustered around her when he found it necessary to put them, none too gently, out of his way.

She saw him coming toward her and her face lit up. It was as if the sun came out in a world that had been doomed to gray.

But he could not let her worm into his heart just like that!

"What the hell do you think you're doing?" he demanded when he finally reached her. He folded his arms over his chest and gazed down at her.

Her expression turned from warmly welcoming to mutinous in a split second.

"Pardon?" she said snootily.

"You heard me."

"I'm racing in the novice division today," she said. "Leo and I have been working on it all week. Haven't we, Leo?"

"Darned right," Leo said, eyeing Luke stubbornly and folding his own arms over his rather massive chest. He was aging, but he still looked tough as nails and had all the tattoos to prove it. "You got something to say about that?"

"It's between me and Maggie," Luke said.

"Leo's my coach," she told him, "and you are not the boss over me, Luke August."

He stared at her, stunned. Was that not the exact emotion he had felt when he had shown her the entry form for this very race and she had expressed her disapproval?

He had never had the tables turned on him so thoroughly, and he was not happy about it. In fact, he felt furious.

"You are riding in this race over my dead body," he said.

He said it even though he knew it was exactly the wrong thing to say. He said it even though he knew if someone had ever worded a request like that to him, he would have done the exact opposite just for spite.

But Maggie wasn't spiteful, like he was. Or stubborn.

Though from the look on her face, he realized he didn't know half of what there was to know about Maggie.

He wasn't willing to risk her at this stage. She could be hurt out there. She could be killed. What had Leo been thinking, taking her on as a pupil?

Luke had seen her ride. She had no aptitude for sports. She had no competitive spirit, no athletic ability.

"I am riding in this race," she told him, her face set in stubborn lines.

Leo clapped her approvingly on the shoulder. A few of the other guys, listening avidly though it was obviously none of their business, also murmured approvingly. Luke glared until most of them got the hint that they might be standing in the danger zone and disappeared.

"We need a moment alone," he told Leo.

Leo looked to Maggie for the okay. For a woman who had never been terrific at the man-woman interchanges, it occurred to Luke she had won over every male here without half trying! She thought over his request for a moment alone and finally nodded, but reluctantly.

"Are you sure?" Leo asked her, and then something caught the corner of his eye and his head swivelled away from his star pupil. "Ooh, la, la," he said. "What have we here?"

Luke couldn't have cared less, but he glanced the way Leo was looking—and closed his eyes and groaned.

Here came his mother. She was actually wearing blue jeans, rhinestone-studded, with stiletto heels and a silk blouse, diamonds dripping from her ears.

Luke wished he had warned her about the earrings.

"Luke," she called, giving him a little wave.

"You know the babe?" Leo said, a little too lasciviously for Luke's liking.

"She's my mother," Luke said, part resignation and part warning. And she couldn't have picked a worse time to turn up, either.

Still, he made introductions. Maggie was acting as if they were not in the middle of a most important discussion. She and his mother were eyeing each other with the frightening enthusiasm of people who knew they were going to know each other for a long, long time.

"My dear," his mother said to Maggie, "you are everything I had hoped for for Luke. Everything."

Maggie blushed. He glared at his mother. For God's sake. She had known Maggie fifteen seconds. How could she say such a thing?

He glanced at Maggie and saw how his mother could say such a thing. And saw why all the guys who hung around the dirt track were so taken with her.

That faint uncertainty that Maggie had always carried with her was gone. She had come into her own in a big way since he had seen her last. She looked more than gorgeous. More than confident. She looked absolutely genuine. And there was nothing more attractive in the world than that—someone who had learned to be themselves, and liked what they had found.

He thought of how good he was at pretending to be other people. Why was that? Was it because he was in some way dissatisfied with who he was?

That was the problem with loving a woman like Maggie. He had succeeded in living his life on the surface, and she made him go deeper. Without half trying she made him come face-to-face with who he was. They were supposed to be arguing about whether or not she was racing, and instead he was getting sidetracked into an entirely unexplored area of his psyche.

"I simply can't wait to get to know you better, Maggie," his mother was saying.

It occurred to Luke if he didn't cut her off at the pass, his mother was going to propose for him. He wondered, stunned if that was what he planned to do. Did he plan to marry Maggie?

Damned right, the voice of his reason told him, most unreasonably.

Well, maybe eventually, after he got Maggie sorted out about the race. "Leo, would you go buy my mother a soda? Maggie and I have business to discuss."

Leo apparently forgot he was Maggie's coach and defender, because he offered his elbow to Luke's mother with old-world courtliness. "Annie?"

Luke had never heard anyone call his mother anything but Annabelle. But his mother giggled girlishly, looped her arm through Leo's and allowed herself to be led away.

"Good grief," Luke moaned, watching them go.

"Luke," Maggie said, "your mother is so adorable. And aren't she and Leo cute together?"

"Don't even try and sidetrack me," he said. His mother was not adorable! And Leo couldn't be cute if he put on a fuzzy pink bear suit.

"Sidetrack you?" she returned innocently. "Luke, I don't know what you mean."

"Okay," Luke told her in a low voice. "You've made your point. I get it."

"You do?" she asked, all wide-eyed innocence.

"Oh, sure. I get exactly how I've made people feel all these years. I understand how I made you feel when I told you I was entering this race over your better judgment. I'm sorry I made you feel that way. I'm sorry you worried needlessly. So, here's the deal. You win. I won't race. You won't race."

She smiled rather tragically, as if he was an idiot child who wasn't quite getting it.

"I don't think that would be a win for either of us," she said.

"What?" he sputtered, not sure he could have possibly heard her correctly.

"I am racing. You can do whatever you want."

"Maggie! This has gone far enough."

"No," she said, "it hasn't. All my life, Luke, I've played it safe. I've never taken chances. I've never been bold and daring. I thought I could protect myself from being hurt that way. But you know what? I was wrong. All I did was stop myself from living."

"Maggie," he said, leaning very close, his mouth practically at her ear, "I love you. If something ever happened to you, it would feel as though the sun set on my world forever."

She tilted her head back and looked at him. A light came on in her eyes. Her lips captured his.

He was aware of the guys cheering around them, but only faintly, as he concentrated on the kiss. He was sure his declaration of love had convinced her. Instead, she let go of his lips and smiled at him.

"Love lets go," she said. "It doesn't hang on."

It seemed as though he had waited his whole life to hear a woman capable of saying those words to him.

But now that he had heard them, in this context, he was not so sure that they were what he wanted to hear after all.

Still, he looked at the light shining in her eyes and knew she was right. She had played it safe her whole life. She had made some trade-offs that she had paid too much for. Now she was prepared to take some risks. And he realized he was part of her risk-taking package.

He knew what he had to do, and what he had to say.

He knew love was requiring more of him.

He took a step back from her. "Good luck," he said hoarsely.

"You, too," she said. She smiled, lowered the visor over her face and turned on the machine. To the cheers of her dedicated fans, she putted off for her practice run around the novice track.

Distracted, Luke went and got ready for his own race. He felt as if he was reeling, had none of the kind of focus that was required to make a competitive run.

The start of his own race was called. He pulled into his place.

The starting flag swept down and for the first time in his life he was aware of holding back, of having a responsibility larger than feeding his own need. For the first time in his life he held something back as he made his way around the track.

And he paid for it. At the end of the race, he came in fourth. But he was aware, as he crossed the finish line, that he did not feel disappointed with his result. Instead, Luke August was aware of a sensation of freedom unlike any he had ever felt.

For once in his life he had not needed the win to make him feel good. What was making him feel good, that place inside him filled to overflowing for the first time in his life, was love.

He joined Billy and Nurse Wagner in the stands just in time to watch Maggie's race. His mother and Leo came over and joined them.

His mother made a great fuss over Billy and, rather than be embarrassed by it, Billy seemed to take to her like a duck to water.

Luke had a feeling something very special would happen between those two. His mother was looking for a child to love, to make up for one she felt she had not loved enough a long, long time ago. And here was a boy who needed all the love he could get. It was a match made in heaven.

Nurse Wagner was no dummy, either. "Annabelle," she said, "do you ever do volunteer work?"

"Oh, I used to. Silly things," his mother said.

They began talking like the oldest of friends. Leo, the newest of friends, looked faintly chagrined by it all.

Luke returned his focus to the racers lining up at the start. Leo, who suddenly seemed to realize his star was out there, glanced at Luke, and together they left the stands to get a place closer to the track.

There were eight novices in the race. Maggie was wearing the number twelve. Luke had to fight back a primal urge to protect her, to run out there and pull her off that bike and drag her off to safety, by her hair if necessary. But he fought down the caveman. And watched.

The flag went down.

It was so loud on the track, Maggie felt disoriented. Her nerves were eating her alive. But she did see the flag go down. She seemed to forget every single thing Leo had drummed into her over the last week. Nothing could have prepared her for the amount of noise and then the blinding cloud of dust as the other competitors leaped off the starting line.

It was not helping that the last thing she had seen was Luke coming closer to the track, his brow knotted with worry, his emotion on his sleeve.

The man was crazy in love with her!

The thought filled her with a wild and surging energy. She gunned her motorcycle, felt the little lift of the front end that meant she had given it a bit too much, and settled into the business at hand. Now she could remember everything Leo had told her.

She felt as if she were entering a place of heightened awareness. She was totally aware of the track, the other racers, her own body and the capabilities of the bike beneath her. There was a glorious sense of being connected to all things, of being totally in the moment. No wonder Luke loved this sport.

Still, despite her great effort she drifted farther and farther behind the other racers. She just did not have the aggressive edge she needed, the pull-out-all-stops attitude.

She finished the race dead last.

She took off her helmet sheepishly, to find Leo and Luke right there, both of them beaming as though she had won the race instead of lost it.

And that was when Maggie understood. Taking a risk wasn't about winning or losing. It was about living.

She looked at the tenderness and relief in Luke's eyes. He lifted her off that bike and swung her around as if she was light as a feather.

She knew she was ready, finally, to take the greatest risk of all.

His mother arrived, and Billy and Hillary.

"I'd like to take you all to my club for dinner," his mother announced. "You, too, Leo."

Maggie sent Luke a private and frantic look. He interpreted it exactly.

"How about if we meet you there?" he asked. His

mother named the time, and he took Maggie's elbow and they ran toward her Volkswagen.

"We'll come back later for my truck and bike," he said.

"Your place is closer," she said when he took the downtown Portland route.

"You don't want to meet my new roommate," he said.

She slugged him playfully on the arm. "Let me guess? Bambi? Tiffany? Star?"

He laughed. "Stinkbomb, Too." And he told her about his pathetic effort to replace her with a puppy.

They were still laughing when they entered her apartment.

"Have you ever showered with a man, Maggie Mouse?" he asked her softly.

She felt suddenly shy and scared. "No."

"It's a breeze compared to what you just did out there. Trust me."

And she realized she did. She trusted him completely, more than she had ever trusted another living soul.

When they went into her tiny bathroom, for some reason Maggie noticed the NoWait on the counter by the sink. She realized that she had not used it for a full week, her life full to brimming with the new adventure she had chosen.

Even without NoWait, the new Maggie, bold and beautiful, had emerged. And beauty had turned out to be about finding her strength, and giving herself over to risk. It hadn't had one darn thing to do with being skinnier. She leaned over slightly, and unnoticed by Luke, she pushed the NoWait off the counter and into the bin. She realized she did not want to be one bit different than she was right this instant.

In moments their dirty clothes were in a pile on the bathroom floor, and they were cloaked in the steam of the shower. Maggie was not sure she had ever experienced an intimacy so thrilling as Luke's strong, sure hands on her body, slipping over her. The dust and grime and sweat from the track washed away, leaving her feeling fresh and new and on fire for him all over again. Being away from him for a week had made her so hungry for him she felt that she could die from it.

She touched his wet skin and marveled how its texture could be so totally different wet than dry. She slid her hands over him, and then he pulled her close and kissed her hard. Even his kisses tasted different in the shower.

The water turned suddenly cold, but it didn't put out the fire. Not even close. Luke slammed the shower valve closed with his foot, then quickly dealt with the faucets. Then he picked her up and took her to bed.

"Have I told you yet that I love you?" he whispered as he put her slippery body in the bed, climbed in beside her and pulled the sheet over them both.

"As a manipulative tool only," she reminded him. "Using it to try and get me not to race."

"Okay. I love you." He kissed the top of her head. "I love you." He burrowed under the sheet and kissed the instep of her foot. "I love you." He kissed her belly button.

"Are you still being manipulative?" she asked breathlessly.

"Oh, yeah," he answered, his voice a rasp.

She laughed. "I think I know what you want this time."

"I better just make sure you know what I want." He kissed her ear. "I love you." He kissed her inner thigh. "I love you."

He kissed every nameable part of her body and some unnamed. And then he captured her mouth. "I love you, Miss Maggie. I want you to marry me."

She felt the breath whoosh out of her body. Somehow, when she had decided to accept a life with more risk, she had accepted a philosophy of living moment for moment, with no attachment to results, no looking to the future for contentment.

And now Luke was holding out a glimpse of a shining future. Of days drenched in the sunlight of his love and his kisses. Of days of laughter and adventure.

Of days when the only adventure would be being together, doing nothing special, laughing over small things. Like green-eyed boys with freckles and messy hair.

She began to cry helplessly.

"Don't cry, Maggie," he whispered. "We're just getting to the good part." He kissed a few more body parts. Soon she forgot to cry.

But she began again, half an hour later, secure in the circle of his arms and his love.

"Hey," he said, "stop that." He traced a tear with his fingertip, held it to his lip and tasted it. Was it possible for tears to taste of honey instead of salt?

"I just feel so happy. I just feel so grateful for every single event of my life leading me to this. Even being left at the altar."

"I'm still going to rearrange his face if I ever meet him."

"No, you aren't, Luke. You're going to thank him for setting me free to find you."

He was silent for a long moment. And then he said, "Maggie, all my life I've looked at things one way. It was cut and dried. You make me look at the world differently. You make me feel different. All my life I've enjoyed pretending to be other people. I'd make a game out of it. It was funny. But right underneath the laughter was a dissatisfaction with who I was.

"Do you know that lying here with you is the first time I can remember being absolutely content with who I am? I didn't even have to win my race today to feel that."

"Do you think you can be absolutely content going out to dinner, because—" she pointed at the clock "—we're going to be late."

"Let's cancel."

"It seemed as if it would mean a lot to your mother. And Billy won't be comfortable if we aren't there."

"Miss Maggie, you are determined to make me a better man."

As he said the words, Luke saw himself in her eyes. He hoped he could always live up to what he saw there. A man who was larger than he was before, a better man, a man capable of forgiveness.

"Wear your red dress," he growled at Maggie.

"I wouldn't wear any other."

By the time Maggie got dressed and they'd stopped at his house for him to change, they were considerably late to his mother's dinner party.

The club was unchanged from the days he had been forced to come here as a child. The dining room was terribly formal, dark oak paneling with white linen tablecloths. And there was his mother, sitting at the head of the table, holding court with Leo and Hillary and Billy, looking like the queen in her diamond earrings and a pure white dress.

He wished they'd gone for pizza.

But he didn't say anything, because when she saw him come in, his mother's face lit with a happiness that was almost otherworldly.

What had he ever done to deserve a light going on like that in two women's faces just because he walked into a room? He went and kissed his mother on the cheek and didn't mention the earrings or her selection of restaurants. He suddenly was aware he didn't want to hurt his mother. The war was over.

Because she was working so hard at accepting him the way he was, and love made him able to see, it was time to return that same courtesy to her.

He was planning to tell them that he and Maggie were getting married, but they had no sooner sat down than his mother turned to him and said, with tears shining in her eyes, "Billy has some wonderful news to share with us."

Billy looked shy and in awe of the surroundings. "My treatments are over for now," he said. "The tests say I'm cancer-free. I'm officially in remission."

They ordered champagne and even Billy got some. Luke exchanged looks with Maggie. Their news could wait for another time.

He looked around the table and could feel the force of love shimmering in the air around them. He took Maggie's hand in his.

Luke had never been a philosophical kind of guy, but sitting at that table, he became aware of the thread that connected each person who sat here. Wasn't all of life about this wondrous thing called hope?

An aging woman hoping to make amends and find

forgiveness. A young boy, his life barely started, hoping for a miracle. Maggie, whose love had been betrayed so brutally and unjustly, hoping that such a thing as real love existed—and willing to bet everything on that single hope.

And Luke? What had he hoped for? He had hoped, in some secret depth within him that there was a place where he would not have to run so hard or so fast. He had hoped there was a place where a man could rest without his loneliness and pain catching up with him.

Each of the people at this table were connected by that thread of hope. Even Leo, who was looking at his mother, and Hillary, looking at Billy.

Each of them believed, in this shining moment, that the miracle had found them.

And the miracle had a name. It was love.

"My mom said I could get a dog when I get home," Billy said happily.

"Oh, boy, do I have a deal for you." Luke didn't really think he needed Stinkbomb, Too, anymore.

A small thing, a boy wanting a dog. But it was the same boy who had been writing his will just a short time ago. Something had changed in him. Billy believed there would be a future after all, and Luke had to put a hand to his eyes at the sudden pricking he felt there.

Hours later they stood on the front steps of his mother's club, saying goodbye to his mother and Leo and Hillary.

It had been a wonderful night, full of laughter and companionship. Maggie had turned every male head in the place.

Billy was between him and Maggie, in his wheelchair looking exhausted, but happy, too. They dropped him off at the hospital, visited for a short time in his room and then left.

Luke opened the front door of the hospital for her, and Maggie joined the swarm of people leaving the hospital as visiting hours ended.

She stopped so suddenly that he bumped into her and nearly knocked her down. Unfazed, she turned into his arms and held him tight.

"What?" he asked her.

"That day we met—the day you ran me down—I saw a couple kissing on these steps."

"Really?"

"Yes. And I was watching them, instead of watching where I was going, and I had hit the door. I was quite dazed from it."

"Not looking where you were going at all," he agreed.

"Luke, if those people hadn't been there, do you think I would have met you?"

"I don't know," he said slowly.

"I judged them at the time. I didn't think they should be behaving like that in public. And at the same time I envied them. I wished I loved someone enough not to care who was watching when I kissed him."

He waited.

"I love someone that much now." She wrapped her hands in his shirt and pulled him toward her.

"Hey!" he teased. "There are all these people watching."

"Who knows?" she whispered. "Maybe there is someone watching right now who needs to see this just as much as I needed to see it. Maybe me kissing you on the front steps of the hospital will set a whole new chain of events into motion that are unpredictable and wild and wonderful."

"So, stop talking and start kissing," he told her. "I'm all for altruism."

She laughed, a devil-may-care laugh that was reckless and endearing and definitely the most delightful sound he had ever heard.

"You're going to like the new me," she said.

"I liked the old you just fine."

"I think you always saw who I really was, Luke," she said, twining her arms around his neck, and sliding her leg up his thigh.

Just like that the world was the two of them, bold and beautiful, and crazy in love.

And he knew it was going to be like that for a long, long time.

Epilogue

Dr. Richard Strong looked at the clock in his office. Eight o'clock. Time to go home. It was a Saturday night. Even someone dedicated beyond reason to his career could not be faulted for going home at eight o'clock on a Saturday night.

But the thought of home made him feel distinctly lonely. It was not really a home. It was an apartment, and it did not actually have much more personality than this office.

It had been a tough week in some ways. His first seminar had ended, and with it had gone all the one-to-one approval he had gotten so accustomed to receiving. When he led The New You: Bold and Beautiful seminar he had felt as if he mattered, had felt important, respected, liked.

He reminded himself that the weight-loss visualization series would be starting soon, but the thought did not lift his spirits.

"Ah, well," he said, giving in to temptation, "let's see what silly Dr. Eatwell has had to say this week."

Richard had taped the shows, Monday to Friday, but had refused to watch them. He had decided "Living Airy with Dr. Terry" was the worst kind of trash. He had sworn off the show completely. He had convinced himself that only common, uneducated people would take pleasure from watching that fat little man hand out advice.

But in some secret part of himself he missed Dr. Terry.

With a kind of guilty pleasure, he plucked Monday's tape from his video cabinet and put it in.

The opening bars of music were playing when he noticed a streetlight reflecting off the television screen. He got up to close his blinds.

His hand froze on the blind string. He couldn't believe what he was seeing. It was Maggie Sullivan in that red dress on the front steps of Portland General, right across the way from his office.

It was definitely Maggie and that mountain of a man, Luke August, who Richard had made the mistake of going to see at his construction site.

Only maybe it had not been a mistake, after all.

For she had stopped and was gazing up at the man, and he was looking back at her. There was no mistaking that look, even from a distance. Those two people were crazy about each other.

And then, without warning, they were holding each other way too tightly. And kissing with mad passion, uncaring that they were blocking the steps, that people were having trouble getting by them, that people were looking at them with reactions that ranged from amusement to envy to disgust.

Slowly, Richard closed the blinds. Really, it should have made him feel lonelier than ever.

But it didn't. He wished, briefly, that he could be free from caring about what people thought of him. It was a prison, really, that he lived in every day.

But on the brighter side, seeing Maggie like that made him feel as if, somehow, he had made a difference. Counted. Hadn't he encouraged Maggie? Hadn't he gone and tried to talk sense to that young man? Hadn't he exposed the worst of his own life experience in trying to help the young couple?

He took a seat on the couch and reminded himself that Cynthia Reynolds was here in Portland, willing to try NoWait and signed up for one of his seminars.

With Cynthia's endorsement, he had no doubt a whole world beyond Portland could be opening to him soon. The loneliness evaporated, and feeling strangely content, with something to hope for, Richard used the remote to turn up the sound on Dr. Terry Beachball.

* * * * *

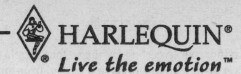

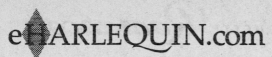

SILHOUETTE *Romance*®

Escape to a place where a kiss is still a kiss...

Feel the breathless connection...

*Fall in love as though it were
the very first time...*

Experience the power of love!

Come to where favorite authors—such as

Diana Palmer, Stella Bagwell, Marie Ferrarella

*and many more—deliver modern fairy tale
romances and genuine emotion,
time after time after time....*

*Silhouette Romance—
from today to forever.*

Live the possibilities

Harlequin Historicals®
Historical Romantic Adventure!

From rugged lawmen and valiant knights to defiant heiresses and spirited frontierswomen, Harlequin Historicals will capture your imagination with their dramatic scope, passion and adventure.

Harlequin Historicals... they're too good to miss!

HARLEQUIN®
INTRIGUE®

WE'LL LEAVE YOU BREATHLESS!

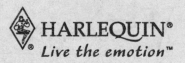

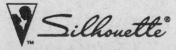